# THE CALL OF THE WILDFLOWER

Henry S. Salt

# The Call of the Wildflower

EMMA
STERN
PUBLISHING

## Emma Stern Publication

ISBN: 978-1-911224-19-8

*This edition published in 2016*

Emma Stern Publishing
107 Fleet Street
London
EC4A 2AB

**www.emmastern.com**
www.facebook.com/emmasternpublishing
Email: editorial@emmastern.com
Email: marketing@emmastern.com

Printed in Great Britain

# Contents

# I
## THE CALL OF THE WILDFLOWER

THE "call of the wild," where the love of flowers is concerned, has an attraction which is not the less powerful because it is difficult to explain. The charm of the garden may be strong, but it is not so strong as that which draws us to seek for wildflowers in their native haunts, whether of shore or water-meadow, field or wood, moorland or mountain. A garden is but a "zoo" (with the cruelty omitted); and just as the true natural history is that which sends us to study animals in the wilds, not to coop them in cages, so the true botany must bring man to the flower, not the flower to man.

That the lovers of wildflowers—those, at least, who can give active expression to their love—are not a numerous folk, is perhaps not surprising; for even a moderate knowledge of the subject demands such favourable conditions as free access to nature, with opportunities for observation beyond what most persons command; but what they lack in numbers they make up in zeal, and to none is the approach of spring more welcome than to those who are then on the watch for the reappearance of floral friends.

For it is as friends, not garden captives or herbarium specimens, that the flower-lover desires to be acquainted with flowers. It is not their uses that attract him; *that* is the business of the herbalist. Nor is it their structure and analysis; the botanist will see to that. What he craves is a knowledge of the loveliness, the actual life and character of plants in their relation to man—what may be called the spiritual aspect of flowers—and this is seen and felt much more closely when they are sought in their free wild state than when they are cultivated on rockery or in parterre.

The reality of this love of wildflowers is evident, but its cause and meaning are less easy to discern. Is it only part of a modern "return to nature," or a sign of some latent sympathy between plant and man? We do not know; but we know that our interest in flowers is no longer utilitarian, as in the herbalism of a bygone time, or decorative and æsthetic, as in the immemorial use of the garland on festive occasions, and in the association of the wine-cup with the rose. The "great affection" that Chaucer felt for the daisy marked a new era; and later poets have carried the sentiment still further, till it reached a climax in the faith that Wordsworth avowed:

One impulse from a vernal wood
May teach you more of man,
Of moral evil and of good,
Than all the sages can.

Here is a new herbalism—of the heart. We smile nowadays at the credulity of the old physicians, who rated so highly the virtues of certain plants as to assert, for example, that comfrey—the "great consound," as they called it—had actual power to unite and solidify a broken bone. But how if there be flowers that can in very truth make whole a broken spirit? Even in the Middle Ages it was recognized that mental benefit was to be gained from this source, as when betony was extolled for its value in driving away despair, and when *fuga dæmonum* was the name given to St. John's-wort, that golden-petalled amulet which, when hung over a doorway, could put all evil spirits to flight. That, like many another flower, it can put "the blues" to flight, is a fact which no modern flower-lover will doubt.

But what may be called the anthropocentric view of wildflowers is now happily becoming obsolete. "Their beauty was given them for our delight," wrote Anne Pratt in one of the pleasantest of her books: "God sent them to teach us lessons of Himself." It would somewhat spoil our joy in the beauty of wildflowers if we thought they had been "sent," like potted plants from a nursery, for any purpose whatsoever; for it is their very naturalness, their independence of man, that charms us, and our regard for them is less the prosaic satisfaction of an owner in his property, than the love of a friend, or even the worship of a devotee:

The devotion to something afar

From the sphere of our sorrow.

This, I think, is the true gospel of the love of flowers, though as yet it has found but little expression in the literature of the subject. "Flowers as flowers," was Thoreau's demand, when he lamented in his journal that there was no book which treated of them in that light, no real "biography" of plants. The same want is felt by the English reader to-day: there is no writer who has done for the wildflower what Mr. W. H. Hudson has done for the bird.

Indeed, the books mostly fail, not only to portray the life of the plant, but even to give an intelligible account of its habitat and appearance; for very few writers, however sound their technical knowledge, possess the gift of lucid description—a gift which depends, in its turn, upon that sympathy with other minds which enables an author to see precisely what instruction is needed. Thus it often happens that, unless personal help is available, it is a matter of great difficulty for a beginner to learn the haunts of flowers, or to

9

distinguish them when found; for when he refers to the books he finds much talk about inessential things, and little that goes directly to the point.

One might have thought that a new and strange flower would attract the eye more readily than a known one, but it is not so; the old is detected much more easily than the new. "Out of sight, out of mind," says the proverb; and conversely that which is not yet in mind will long tarry out of sight. But when once a new flower, even a rare one, has been discovered, it is curious how often it will soon be noticed afresh in another place: this, I think, must be the experience of all who have made systematic search for flowers, and it explains why the novice will frequently see but little where the expert will see much.

Not until the various initial obstacles have been overcome can one appreciate the true "call of the wild," the full pleasures of the chase. When we have learnt not only what plants are to be looked for, but those two essential conditions, the *when* and the *where*; the rule of season and of soil; the flowers that bloom in spring, in summer, or in autumn; the flowers that grow by shore, meadow, bog, river, or mountain; on chalk, limestone, sand, or clay—then the quest becomes more effective, and each successive season will add materially to our widening circle of acquaintance.

Then, too, we may begin to discard that rather vapid class of literature, the popular flower-book, which too often deals sentimentally in vague descriptions of plants, diversified with bad illustrations, and with edifying remarks about the goodness of the Creator, and may find a new and more rational interest in the published *Floras* of such counties or districts as have yet received that distinction. For dry though it is in form, a *Flora*, with its classified list of plants, and its notes collected from many sources, past and present, as to their "stations" in the county, becomes an almost romantic book of adventure, when the student can supply the details from his own knowledge, and so read with illumination "between the lines." Here, let us suppose it to be said, is a locality where grows some rare and beautiful flower, one of the prizes of the chase. What hopes and aspirations such an assurance may arouse! What encouragement to future enterprise! What regrets, it may be, for some almost forgotten omission in the past, which left that very neighbourhood unsearched! It is possible that a cold, matter-of-fact entry in a local *Flora* will thus throw a sudden light on some bygone expedition, and show us that if we had but taken a slightly different direction in our walk—but it is vain to lament what is irreparable!

Of such musings upon the might-have-been I can myself speak with feeling, for I was not so fortunate in my youth as to be initiated into the knowledge of flowers: it was not till much later in life, as I wandered among the Welsh and English mountains, that the scales fell from my eyes, and looking on the beauty of the saxifrages I realized what glories I had missed. Thus I was compelled to put myself to school, so to speak, and to make a study of wildflowers with the aid of such books as were available, a process which, like a botanical Jude the Obscure, I found by no means easy. The self-educated man, we know, is apt to be perverse and opinionated; so I trust my readers will make due allowance if they notice such faults in this book. I can truly plead, as the illiterate do, that "I'm no scholar, more's the pity." But it was my friends and acquaintances—those, at least, who had some botanical knowledge—who were the chief sufferers during this period of inquiry; and, looking back, I often marvel

11

at the patience with which they endured the problems with which I confronted them. I remember waylaying my friend, W. J. Jupp, a very faithful flower-lover, with some mutilated and unrecognizable labiate plant which I thought might be calamint, and how tactfully he suggested that my conjecture was "near enough." On another occasion it was Edward Carpenter, the Sage of Millthorpe, or Wild Sage, as some botanical friend once irreverently described him, who volunteered to assist me, by means of a scientific book which shows, by an unerring process, how to eliminate the wrong flowers, until at the end you are left with the right one duly named. All through the list we went; but there must have been a slip somewhere; for in the conclusion one thing alone was clear—that whatever my plant might be, it was not that which the scientific book indicated. Of all my friends and helpers, Bertram Lloyd, whose acquaintance with wildflowers is unusually large, and to whom, in all that pertains to natural history, I am as the "gray barbarian" (*vide* Tennyson) to "the Christian child," was the most constant and long-suffering: he solved many of my enigmas, and introduced me to some of his choicest flower-haunts among the Chiltern Hills. In the course of my researches I was sometimes referred for guidance to persons who were known in their respective home-circles as "the botanists of the family," a title which I found was not quite equivalent to that of "the complete botanist." There was one "botanist of the family" who was visibly embarrassed when I asked her the name of a plant that is common on the chalk hills, but is so carelessly described in the books as to be easily confused with other kindred species. She gazed at it long, with a troubled eye, and then, as if feeling that her domestic reputation must at all hazards be upheld, replied firmly: "Hemp-nettle." Hemp-

12

nettle it was not; it was wild basil; but years after, when I began to have similar questions put to myself, I realized how disconcerting it is to be thus suddenly interrogated. It made me understand why Cabinet Ministers so frequently insist that they must have "notice of that Question." With one complete botanist, however, I was privileged to become acquainted, Mr. C. E. Salmon, whose special diocese, so to speak, is the county of Surrey, but whose intimate knowledge of wildflowers extends to many counties and coasts. Not a few favours did I receive from him, in certifying for me some of the more puzzling plants; and very good-naturedly he bore the disappointment when, on his asking me to send him, for his *Flora of Surrey*, a list of the rarer flowers in the neighbourhood where I was living, I included among them the small bur-parsley (*caucalis daucoides*), a vanished native, a prodigal son of the county, whose return would have been a matter for gladness. But alas, my plant was not a *caucalis* at all, but a *torilis*, a squat weed of the cornfields, which by its superficial resemblance to its rare cousin had grossly imposed upon my ignorance. It is when he has acquired some familiarity with the ordinary British plants that a flower-lover, thus educated late in life, finds his thoughts turning to the vanished opportunities of the past. I used to speculate regretfully on what I had missed in my early wanderings in wild places; as in the Isle of Skye, where I picked up the eagle's feather, but overlooked the mountain flower; or on Ben Lawers, a summit rich in rare Alpines to which I then was stone-blind; or in a score of other localities which I can scarcely hope to revisit. But time, which heals all things, brought me a sort of compensation for these delinquencies; for with a fuller knowledge of plants I could to some extent reconstruct in imagination the sights that were formerly unseen, and with the eye of faith admire the Alpine forget-me-not on the ridges of Ben Lawers, or the yellow butterwort in the marshes of Skye. Nor was it always in imagination only; for sometimes a friend would send me a rare flower from some distant spot; and then there was pleasure indeed in the opening of the parcel and in anticipating what it might contain—the pasque-flower perhaps, or the wild tulip, or the Adonis, or the golden samphire, or some other of the many local treasures that make glad the flower-lover's heart. The exhibitions of wildflowers that are now held in the public libraries of not a few towns are extremely useful, and often awake a love of nature in minds where it has hitherto been but dormant. A queer remark was once made to me by a visitor at the Brighton show. "This is a good institution," he said. "It saves you from tramping for the flowers yourself." I had not regarded the exhibition in that light; on the contrary, it stimulates many persons to a pursuit which is likely to fascinate them more and more.

For no tramps can be pleasanter than those in quest of wildflowers; especially if one has a fellow-enthusiast for companion: failing that, it is wiser to go alone; for when a flower-lover tramps with someone who has no interest in the pursuit, the result is likely to be discomfiting—he must either forgo his own haltings and deviations, with the probability that he will miss something valuable, or he must feel that he is delaying his friend. In a company, I always pray that their number may be uneven, and that it may not be necessary to march stolidly in pairs, where "one to one is cursedly confined," as Dryden said of matrimony; or worst of all, where one's yoke-fellow may insist, as sometimes happens, on walking "in step," and be forever shuffling his feet as if obeying the commands of some invisible drill-sergeant. It is

14

not with the feet that we should seek harmony, but with the heart. My intention in this book is to speak of the more noteworthy flowers of a few distinctive localities that are known to me, starting from the coast of Sussex, and ascending to the high mountains of Wales and the north-west: I propose also to intersperse the descriptive chapters, here and there with discussions of such special topics as may incidentally arise. And here, at the outset, I was tempted to say a few words about my own favourite flowers—not such universally admired beauties as the primrose, violet, daffodil, hyacinth, forget-me-not, and the others, whose names will readily suggest themselves; for, lovely as they are, it would be superfluous to add to their praises; but rather of some less famous plants, the saints and anchorites of the floral world, the flower-lover's flowers—not the popular, but the best-beloved. On second thoughts, however, I will leave these choicest ones, with a single exception, to be mentioned in their due place and surroundings, and will here name but one of them, a flower which is among the first, not only in the order of merit, but in the order of the seasons.

The greater stitchwort, as writers tell us, is one of "the most ornamental of our early flowers"; but surely it is something more than that. The radiance of those white stars that stud the hedge-banks and road-sides in April and May, is dearer to some of us than many of the more favoured blossoms that poets have sung of. The dull English name quite fails to do justice to the almost ethereal lustre of the flower: the Latin *stellaria* is truer and more expressive. The reappearance of the stitchwort, like that of the orange-tip butterfly, is one of the keenest joys of spring; and one of our keenest regrets in spring is that the stitchwort's flowering-season is so short.

## II
## ON SUSSEX SHINGLES

WHERE should a flower-lover begin his story if not from the sea shore? Earth has been poetically described as "daughter of ocean"; and the proximity of the sea has a most genial and stimulating effect upon its grandchildren the flowers, not those only that are peculiar to the beach, but also the inland kinds. There is no "dead sea" lack of vegetation on our coasts, but a marked increase both in the luxuriance of plants and in their beauty.

Sussex is rich in "shingles"—flat expanses of loose pebbles formerly thrown up by the waves, and now lying well above high-water mark, or even stretching landward for some distance. One might have expected these stony tracts to be barren in the extreme; in fact they are the nursery-ground of a number of interesting flowers, including some very rare ones; and in certain places, where the stones are intersected by banks of turf, the eye is surprised by a veritable garden in the wilderness. Let us imagine ourselves on one of these shingle-beds in the early summer, when the show of flowers is at its brightest: and first at Shoreham—"Shoreham, crowned with the grace of years," as Swinburne described it.

Alas! the Shoreham beach, which until less than twenty years ago was in a natural state, has been so overbuilt with ship-works and bungalows that it has become little else than a suburb of Brighton; yet even now the remaining strip of shingle, stretching for half a mile between sea and harbour, is the home of some delightful plants. In the more favoured spots the gay mantle thrown over the stony strand is visible at the first glance in a wonderful blending of colours—the gold of horned poppy, stonecrop, melilot, and kidney vetch; the white of sea-campion; the delicate pink of thrift; and the fiery reds and blues of the gorgeous viper's bugloss—and when a nearer scrutiny is made, a number of minute plants will be found growing in close company along the grassy ridges. The most attractive of these are the graceful little spring vetch (*vicia lathyroides*), the rue-leaved saxifrage, and that tiny turquoise gem which is apt to escape notice, the dwarf forget-me-not—a trio of the daintiest blossoms, red, white, and blue, that eyes could desire to behold.

Shoreham has long been famous for its clovers; and some are still in great force there, especially the rigid trefoil (*trifolium scabrum*), and its congener, *trifolium striatum*, with which it is often confused, while the better-known hare's-foot also covers a good deal of the ground. But there is a sad tale to tell of the plant which once the chief pride of these shingles, the starry-headed trefoil, a very lovely pink flower fringed with silky hairs, which, though not a native, has been naturalized near the bank of the harbour since 1804, but now, owing to the enclosures made for ship-building works, has been all but exterminated. "This," wrote the author of the *Flora of Sussex* (1907) "is one of the most beautiful of our wildflowers, and is found in Britain at Shoreham only. Fortunately it is very difficult to extirpate any of the *leguminosæ*, and it may therefore be hoped that it may long continue to adorn the beach at Shoreham." The hope seems likely to be frustrated. Among the rubble of concrete slabs, and piles of timber, only three or four tufts of the trefoil were surviving last year, with every likelihood of these also disappearing as the place is further "developed." The second of the Shoreham rarities, the pale yellow vetch (*vicia lutea*) has fared better, owing to its wider range, and is still scattered freely over the yet unenclosed shingles. It is a charming flower; but its doom in Sussex seems to be inevitable, for the bungalows, with their back-yards, tennis-courts, "tradesmen's entrances," and other amenities of villadom, will doubtless continue to encroach upon what was once a wild and unsullied tract.

Still sadder is the fate of the devastated coast on the Brighton side of the harbour-mouth, where the low cliffs that overlook the lagoon from Southwick to Fisher's-gate have long been known to botanists as worthy of some attention. Here, on the grassy escarpment, the rare Bithynian vetch used once to grow, as we learn from Mrs. Merrifield's interesting *Sketch of the Natural History of Brighton* (1860); and here we may still find such plants as the sea-radish, a large coarse crucifer with yellow flowers and queer knotted seed-pods; the blue clary, or wild-sage, running riot in great profusion; the fragrant soft-leaved fennel; the strange star-thistle (*calcitrapa*), so-called from its fancied resemblance to an ancient and diabolical military instrument, the caltrop, an iron ball armed with sharp points, which was thrown on the ground to maim the horses in a cavalry charge; the pale-flowered narrow-leaved flax; and lastly, that rather uncanny shrub of the poisonous nightshade order, with small purple flowers and scarlet berries, which is called the "tea-tree," though the tea which its leaves might furnish would hardly make a palatable brew.

Below these cliffs, on an embankment that divides the waters of the lagoon from the seashore, there still flourishes in plenty the fleshy leaved samphire, once sought after for a pickle, and ever famous through the reference in *King Lear* to "one who gathers samphire, dreadful trade." In this locality there is no dreadful trade, except that of reducing a once pleasant shore to an unsightly slag-heap.

Let me now turn from this melancholy spectacle to those Sussex shingles on which the Admiralty and the contractor have not as yet laid a heavy and ruinous hand. On some of the more spacious of these pebbly beaches, as on that which lies between Eastbourne and Pevensey, the traveller may still experience the feeling expressed by Shelley:

I love all waste
And solitary places, where we taste
The pleasure of believing what we see
Is boundless, as we wish our souls to be.

From Langney Point one looks north-east along a desolate shore, beyond which the ruins of Pevensey Castle are seen in the distance, and the width of the shingly belt between the sea and the high-road is at this point scarcely less than a mile. A scene that is bleak and barren enough in its general aspect; but a search soon reveals the presence of floral treasures, the first of which is a rather rare member of the Pink family, the soapwort, which I had long sought in vain until I met with it growing in abundance close to the outskirts of Eastbourne, where it roots so luxuriantly in the loose shingles as to make one wonder why it is so fastidious elsewhere. Among other noticeable inhabitants of these flats, or of the shallow marshy depressions which they enclose, are hairy crowfoot, catmint, white melilot, stinking groundsel, strawberry-headed trefoil, and candytuft—the last-named a rather unexpected flower in such a place.

Still nearer to the sea, not many yards removed from the spray of the waves at their highest, the wild seakale is plentiful; a stout glabrous cabbage, with thick curly leaves and white cruciferous blossoms, it rises straight out of the bare stones, and thrives exceedingly when the folk who stroll along the shore can so far restrain their destructive tendencies as not to hack and mangle it. In its company, perhaps, or in similar situations, will be seen its first-cousin, the sea-rocket, a quaint and pleasant crucifer with zigzag stems, fleshy leaves, and pale lilac petals. The sea-pea, formerly native near Pevensey, is now hardly to be hoped for.

One of the most naturally attractive spots on the Sussex coast is Cuckmere Haven, near Seaford, a gap in the chalk cliffs, about half a mile in width, through which the river Cuckmere finds a dubious exit to the sea. Were it not for the abomination of the rifle-butts, which sometimes close the shore to the public, no more delectable nook could be desired; and to the flower-lover the little shelf of shingle which forms the beach is full of charm. Here, growing along the grassy margin of brackish pools, and itself so like a flowering grass that a sharp eye is needed to detect it, one may find that singular umbelliferous plant—not at all resembling the other members of its tribe—the slender hare's-ear (*bupleurum tenuissimum*), thin, wiry, dark-green, with narrow lance-like leaves and minute yellow umbels. Nearby, the small sea-heath, one of the prettiest of maritime flowers, makes a dense carpet; on the corner of the adjacent cliff the lesser and rarer sea-lavender (*statice binervosa*) is plentiful, and in the late summer blooms at a considerable height on the narrow ledges.

Pagham "Harbour," a wild estuary of some extent, between Selsey and Bognor, is another locality that has earned a reputation for its flowers, the most remarkable of which is the very local proliferous pink, which has long been

20

known as abundant on that portion of the coast, though elsewhere very infrequent. A pleasant walk of about three miles leads from Bognor to Pagham, along a sandy shore fringed with very luxuriant tamarisk-bushes; and when one reaches the stony reef where further progress is barred by the waters or sand-shoals of the "Harbour," the little pink, which bears a superficial resemblance to thrift, will be seen springing up freely among the pebbles. We are told that only one of its blossoms opens at a time; but this is the sort of statement, often copied from book to book, which is not verified by experience, or to which at least many exceptions must be admitted. What is certain is that the proliferous pink has a considerable share of the distinctive grace of its family, and that the occasion of first encountering it will live in the flower-lover's memory.

I have named but a few—those personally known to me—of the rarer or more characteristic shingle-flowers; and in so wide a field there is always the chance of new discoveries: hence the unfailing interest, to the botanist, of places which, apart from their flora, are likely to be shunned as wearisome. The shore itself is seldom without visitors; but the shingles that stretch back from the shore rarely attract the footsteps even of the hardiest walkers. It is only when there has been a murder in one of those solitary spots—or at least something that the newspapers can describe as "dramatic" or "sensational"—that the holiday-folk in the neighbouring towns forsake for a day or two the pleasures of pier or parade, and sally forth over the stony wildernesses in a search for "clues"; as when the "Crumbles," near Eastbourne, was the scene, two years ago, of a murder, and at a later date of a ghost. To discover the foot of some partially buried victim protruding from the pebbles—*that* is deemed a sufficient object for a pilgrimage. The gold of the sea-poppy and the pink of the thrift are trifles that are passed unseen.

# III
## BY DITCH AND DIKE

"LEVELS," or "brooks," is the name commonly given in Sussex to a number of grassy tracts, often of wide extent, which, though still in a state of semi-wildness, have been so far reclaimed from primitive fens as to afford a rough pasturage for horses and herds of cattle, the ground being drained and intersected by dikes and sluggish streams. In these spacious and unfrequented flats wildfowl of various kinds are often to be seen; herons stand motionless by the pools, or flap slowly away if disturbed in their meditation; pewits wheel and cry overhead; and the redshank, most clamorous of birds during the nesting-season, makes such a din as almost to distract the attention of the intruding botanist. For it is the botanist who is specially drawn to these wild water-ways, where hours may be profitably spent in strolling beside the brooks, with the certainty of seeing many interesting plants and the chance of finding some unfamiliar ones; nor is there anything to mar his enjoyment, except the possible meeting with a bull on a wide arena from which there is no ready exit, save by jumping a muddy ditch or by crossing one of the narrow and precarious planks which do duty as footbridges.

These "levels," though often bordering on a tidal river, are not themselves salt marshes, nor is their flora a maritime one; in that respect they differ from the East-coast fens described by Crabbe in one of his *Tales*, "The Lover's Journey"; a passage which has been praised as one of the best pictures ever given of dike-land scenery. There are lines in it which might be quoted of the Sussex as well as of the Suffolk marsh-meadows; but for me the verses are spoiled by the strangely apologetic tone which the poet assumed in speaking of the local plants:

The few dull flowers that o'er the place are spread
Partake the nature of their fenny bed.

And so on. Did he think that his polite readers expected to hear of sweet peas and carnations beautifying the desolate mud-banks? The "dulness" seems to be—well, not on the part of the flowers. "Dull as ditchwater," they say. But ditchwater flowers are far from dull.

Of Sussex marshes the most extensive are the Pevensey Levels; but the most pleasantly situated are those that lie just south of Lewes, where the valley of the Ouse widens into an oval plain before it narrows again towards Newhaven. From the central part of this alluvial basin the view is very striking all around; for the estuary seems to be everywhere enclosed, except to seaward, by the great smooth slopes of the chalk Downs. On its west side are three picturesque villages, Iford, Rodmell, and Southease, with churches and farms lying on the very verge of the "brooks": at the head, the quaint old houses and castle of Lewes rise conspicuous like a mediæval town.

But to whichever of these watery wastes the flower-lover betakes himself, he will not lack for occupation. One of the first friends to greet him in the early summer, by the Lewes levels, will be the charming *Hottonia*, or "water-violet," as it is misnamed; for though the petals are pink, its yellow eye and general form proclaim it to be of the *primulaceæ*, and "water-primrose" should by preference be its title. There are few prettier sights than a company of these elegant flowers rising clear above the surface, their slender stems bearing whorls of the pink blossoms, while the dark green featherlike leaves remain submerged. This "featherfoil," as it is sometimes called, is as lovely as the primrose of the woods.

Companions or near neighbours of the *Hottonia* are the arrow-head, at once recognized by its bold sagittate leaves, and the frog-bit, another flower of three white petals, whose small reniform foliage, floating on the brooks, gives it the appearance of a dwarf water-lily. By no means common, but growing in profusion where it grows at all, the dainty little frog-bit, once met with, always remains a favourite. The true water-lilies, both the white and the yellow, are also native on the levels; so, too, is the quaint water-milfoil, with its much-cut submerged leaves resembling those of the featherfoil, and its numerous erect flower-spikes dotting the surface of the pools. All these water-nymphs may be seen simultaneously blossoming in June.

More prominent than such small aquatics are the tall-growing kinds which lift their heads two or three feet above the waters. Of these quite the handsomest is the flowering rush (*butomus*), stately and pink-petaled; among the rest are the two water-plantains (the lesser one rather uncommon); the water-speedwell, a gross and bulky *veronica* which lacks the charm of its smaller relative the brook-lime; and the queer mare's-tails, which in the midst of a running stream look like a number of tiny fir-trees out of their element. The umbelliferous family is also well represented. Wild celery is there; and the showy water-parsnip (*sium*); the graceful tubular water-dropwort, and its big neighbour the horse-bane, which in some places swells to an immense size in the centre of the ditches. On the margin grows the pretty trailing money-wort, or "creeping Jenny"; and with it, maybe, the white-blossomed brook-weed, or water-pimpernel, which at first sight has more likeness to the crucifers than to its real relatives the primroses, and is thus apt to puzzle those by whom it has not previously been encountered.

Rambling beside these so-called brooks, which are mostly not brooks but channels of almost stagnant water, one cannot fail to remark the clannishness of many of the flowers: they grow in groups, monopolizing nearly the whole length of a ditch, and making a show by their united array of leaves or blossoms. In one part, perhaps, the slim water-violet predominates; then, as you turn a corner, a long vista of arrow-heads meets the eye, nothing but arrow-heads between bank and bank, their sharp, barbed foliage topping the surface in a phalanx: or again, you may come upon fifty yards of frog-bit, a multitude of small green bucklers that entirely hide the water; or a radiant colony of water-lilies, whose broad leaves make the intrusion of other aquatics scarcely possible, and provide a cool pavement for wagtail and moorhen to walk on. It is noticeable, too, that the lesser water-plantain, unlike the greater, is almost confined to one section of the levels; and in like manner the brook-weed and the burmarigold have each occupied for their headquarters the banks of a particular dike.

The fringed buckbean (*villarsia*) is said to be an inhabitant of these brooks. I have not seen it there; but it may be found, sparsely, in the river Ouse, a short distance above Lewes, where its round leaves float on the quiet backwaters like those of a large frog-bit or a small water-lily, though the botanists tell us it is a gentian. I remember that on the first occasion when I saw it there, on a late summer day, there was only a single blossom left, and as that was on a deep pool, several yards from the bank, there was no choice but to swim for it. The great yellow cress (*nasturtium amphibium*), a glorified cousin of the familiar water-cress, is also native on the Ouse above Lewes, less frequently below.

More spacious than the Lewes levels, but drearier, and on the whole less interesting, are those of Pevensey, which cover a wide tract to the east of Hailsham, formerly an inlet of the sea, where the sites of the few homesteads that rise above the flat meadows, such as Chilley and Horse-eye, were once islands in the bay. Walking north from Pevensey, by a road which traverses this inhospitable flat, one sees the walls of Hurstmonceux Castle in front, on what was originally the coast-line; on either side of the highway is a maze of ditches and dikes, among which rare flowers are to be found, notably the broad-leaved pepperwort, the largest and most remarkable of its family, and the great spearwort, said to be locally plentiful near Hurstmonceux. The bladderwort, reputed common on these marshes, seems to have become much scarcer than it was twenty years back.

For other flowers, other fenny tracts may be sought; Henfield Common, for instance, has the bog-bean, the marsh St. John's-wort, and still better, the marsh-cinquefoil. But of all Sussex water-meadows with which I am acquainted the richest are the Amberley Wild Brooks, which lie below Pulborough, adjacent to the tidal stream of the Arun, a piece of partially drained bog-land which in a wet winter season is apt to be flooded anew, and to revert to its primitive state of swamp. It is a glorious place to wander over, on a sunny August afternoon, with the great escarpment of the Downs, and the ever-prominent Chanctonbury Ring, close in view to the south; and in a long summer day the expedition can be combined with a visit to Arundel Park, only three miles distant, the best of parks, as being the least parklike and most natural, and having a goodly store of the wildflowers that are dwellers upon chalk hills.

The Amberley Wild Brooks possess this great merit, that in addition to most of the aquatics and dike-land plants above-mentioned, they present a fine display of the tall riverside flowers. Their wet hollows that teem with frog-bit, arrow-head, water-parsnip, water-plantain, yellow cress, glaucous stitchwort, and other choice things, are fringed here and there with purple loosestrife, and with marsh-woundwort almost equal to the loosestrife in size and colour; and mingling with these in like luxuriance are yellow loosestrife, tansy, toadflax, and water-ragwort—a brilliant combination of purple flowers and gold. Then, as if the better to set off this spectacle, there is in some places a background of staid and massive herbs like the great water-dock,

And bulrushes, and reeds of such deep green
As soothe the dazzled eye with sober sheen.

One would fear that this wealth of diverse hues might even become embarrassing, were it not that the heart of the flower-lover is insatiable.

# IV
## LIKENESSES THAT BAFFLE

ONE of the first difficulties by which those who would learn their native flora are beset is the likeness which in some cases exists between one plant and another—not the close resemblance of kindred species, such as that found, for instance, among the brambles or the hawkweeds, which is necessarily a matter for expert discrimination, but the superficial yet often puzzling similarity in what botanists call the "habit" of wildflowers. Thus the horse-shoe vetch may easily be mistaken, by a beginner, for the bird's-foot trefoil, or the field mouse-ear chickweed for the greater stitchwort; and the differences between the dove's-foot crane's-bill and the less common *geranium pusillum* are not at first sight very apparent. Distinguishing features instantly recognized by an expert, who has taken, so to speak, finger-tip impressions of the plants, do not readily present themselves to the layman, whose only guide is the general testimony of structure, colour, and height.

It is, moreover, unfortunate that some of the popular flower-books, owing to the slovenly way in which their descriptions are worded, are of little help; they not only fail to give the needed particulars where there is a real likeness, but often, where there is none, create confusion in the reader's mind by depicting quite dissimilar plants in almost identical terms. In Johns's *Flowers of the Field* (edition of 1908), for example, the description of hedge-woundwort hardly differs verbally from that of black horehound, and might certainly mislead a novice who was studying hedgerow flowers. The same writer had an exasperating habit of repeatedly stating that various plants are "well distinguished" by certain features, when in fact it is very difficult, from the accounts given by him, to distinguish them at all!

An earlier and better writer, Anne Pratt, did make an effort in her *Haunts of the Wild Flowers* to indicate the chief characteristics, as between the sea-plantain and the sea-arrowgrass, the hemp-agrimony and the valerian; but even she, when some of the labiate flowers were in question, dismissed them, not very helpfully, as "all growing in abundance, but so much alike that it needs a knowledge of botany to distinguish them from each other"! I have known a case where, owing to a picturesque but inaccurate account, in the same book, the Welsh stonecrop (*sedum Forsterianum*) was confused with the marsh St. John's-wort, which has leaves that bear a curious resemblance to those of the *sedum* tribe.

Even writers of botanical handbooks seem not to realize with what difficulties the uninitiated are faced, in regard to certain groups of plants where the several species, though quite distinct, bear a strong family likeness. The chamomiles, for instance, might well receive some special treatment in books; for it is no simple matter to assign their proper names to some four or five of the clan—the true chamomile, the wild chamomile, the corn chamomile, the stinking chamomile, and the "scentless" mayweed, which is *not* scentless. Many of the umbellifers also are notoriously difficult to identify; and among leguminous plants there is a bewildering similarity between black medick, or "nonsuch," and the lesser clover (*trifolium minus*), which in turn is liable to be confused with the popular hop-clover or with the slender and fairy-like *trifolium filiforme*. "Small examples of *t. minus*," said a well-known botanist, Mr. H. C. Watson, "are so frequently misnamed *t. filiforme*, that I trust only my own eyes for it." "As like as two peas" is a saying which finds fulfilment in these and other examples.

The clovers are indeed a perplexing family; and it is not surprising that the identification of the "shamrock" has given cause for dispute. Two of the smaller trefoils, for example, *trifolium scabrum* and *striatum*, so closely resemble each other that a novice fails to appreciate the assurance given in the *Flora of Kent* that they "can very easily be separated." It is doubtless easy to separate one twin from another twin, Dromio of Ephesus from Dromio of Syracuse, when once you know how to do so; but until you have acquired that knowledge there is material for a "comedy of errors." The majority of folk are much more apt to confuse plants than to distinguish them: witness such names as "fool's-parsley" and "fool's-watercress." Fools there are; yet anyone who has spent time in studying wildflowers, with no better aid than that of the popular books on the subject, will hesitate to pass judgment on such folly; for as so good an observer as Richard Jefferies said: "If you really wish to identify with certainty, and have no botanist friend and no *magnum opus* of Sowerby to refer to, it is very difficult indeed to be quite sure." We have to be thankful for small mercies in this matter; and it may be recognized that in some cases—generally where the similarity is *not* great, as that between the strawberry-leaved cinquefoil and the wild strawberry, or between the feverfew and the scentless mayweed—the books occasionally give a word of advice to "the young botanist." Nine times out of ten, however, that young fellow, or perchance old fellow (for one may be young as a botanist, while by no means young in years), must shift for himself; and doing so, he will gradually learn by experience what a number of likenesses there are among plants, and how many mistakes may be made before a sure acquaintance is arrived at.

The name of "mockers" is sometimes given by gardeners to weeds that are so like certain valued plants as to be easily mistaken for them; and in the same way, in the search for wildflowers, one's attention is often distracted, as, for instance, if one is looking for the spineless meadow-thistle, the eye may be baffled by innumerable knapweed blossoms of the same hue; the clustered bell-flower will feign to be the autumnal gentian, its neighbour on the chalk downs; or the blossoms and leaves of the purple saxifrage on the high mountains are aped by the ubiquitous wild thyme.

Of all these likenesses the most perilous is that between the malodorous ramsons, which have a very abiding smell of garlic, and the highly esteemed lily of the valley. Hence a story which I once heard from the affable keeper who presides over a wooded hill in Westmorland where the lily of the valley abounds, and where visitors are permitted to pick as many flowers as they like after payment of a shilling. Seeing a gentleman busily engaged in gathering a large bunch of ramsons, the keeper, suspecting error, asked him what he supposed himself to be picking. "Why, lilies of the valley, of course," was the reply. When the truth was explained, the visitor thanked the keeper cordially, and added: "I was picking the flowers for my wife: but if I had brought her a present of garlic she would have had something to say to me. I myself have lost the sense of smell."

Likeness or unlikeness—it is all a matter of observation. To a stranger, every sheep in the flock has a face like that of her fellows: to the shepherd there are no two sheep alike.

# V

## BOTANESQUE

AMONG the difficulties that waylay the beginner must be reckoned the botanical phraseology. We have heard of "the language of flowers," and of its romantic associations; but the language of botany is another matter, and though less picturesque is equally cryptic and not to be mastered without study.

When, for example, we read of a certain umbelliferous plant that its "cremocarp consists of two semicircular-ovoid mericarps, constricted at the commissure"—or when, with our lives in our hands, so to speak, we experiment in fungus-eating, and learn that a particular mushroom has its stem "fistulose, subsquamulose, its pileus membranaceous, rarely subcarnose, when young ovato-conic, then campanulate, at length torn and revolute, deliquescent, and clothed with the flocculose fragments of the veil"—we probably feel that some further information would be welcome.

A friend who had been reading a series of articles on botany once remarked to me that "they could scarcely be said to be written in any known language, but were in a new tongue which might perhaps be called Botanesque."

But it is of the botanesque nomenclature that I now wish to speak. The faculty of bestowing appropriate names is at all times a gift, an inspiration, most happy when least laboured, and often eluding the efforts of learned and scientific men. By schoolboys it is sometimes exhibited in perfection; as in a case that I remember at a public school, where three brothers of the name of Berry were severally known, for personal reasons, as Bilberry, Blackberry, and Gooseberry, the fitness of which botanical titles was never for a moment impugned.

But botanists rarely invent names so well. The nomenclature of plants, like that of those celestial flowers, the stars, is a queer jumble of ancient and modern, classical learning and mediæval folk-lore, in which the really characteristic features are often overlooked. In this respect the Latin names are worse offenders than the English; and one is sometimes tempted, in disgust at their pedantic irrelevance, to ignore them altogether, and to exclaim with the poet:

What's in a name? That which we call a rose
By any other name would smell as sweet.

But this would be an error; for a name does greatly enhance the interest of an object, be it boy, or bird, or flower; and the Greek and Latin plant-names, cumbrous and far-fetched though many of them are—as when the saintfoin is absurdly labelled *onobrychis*, on the supposition that its scent provokes an ass to bray—form, nevertheless, a useful link between botanists of different nations and a safeguard against the confusion that arises from a variety of local terms.

Among the English names also there are some clumsy appellations, and in a few cases the Latin ones are much pleasanter: *stellaria*, for example, as I have already said, is more elegant than "stitchwort." "What have I done?" asks the small cousin of the woodruff, in Edward Carpenter's poem, when it justly protests against its hideous christening by man:

What have I done? Man came,
Evolutional upstart one,

35

With the gift of giving a name
To everything under the sun.
What have I done? Man came
(They say nothing sticks like dirt),
Looked at me with eyes of blame,
And called me "Squinancy-wort."

But on the whole the English names of flowers are simpler and more suggestive than the Latin; certainly "monk's-hood" is preferable to *aconitum*, "rest-harrow" to *ononis*, "flowering rush" to *butomus*; and so on, through a long list: and it therefore seems rather strange that the native titles should sometimes be ousted by the foreign. I have met botanists who had quite forgotten the English, and were obliged to ask me for the scientific term before they could sufficiently recall the plant of which we were speaking.

The prefix "common" is often very misleading in the English nomenclature. Anyone, for example, who should go confidently searching for the "common hare's-ear" would soon find that he had got his work cut out. There are, in fact, not many plants that are everywhere common; most of those that are so described should properly be classed as *local*, because, while plentiful in some districts, they are infrequent in others.

Botanical names fall mainly into three classes, the medicinal, the commemorative, the descriptive. The old uses of plants by the herbalists mark the prosaic origin of many of the names; some of which, such as "goutweed," at once explain themselves, as indicating supposed remedies for ills that flesh is heir to. Others, if less obvious, are still not far to seek; the "scabious," for example, derived from the Latin *scabies*, was reputed to be a cure for leprosy: a few, like "eye-bright" (*euphrasia*, gladness), have a more cheerful significance. When we turn to such titles as *centaurea*, for the knapweed and cornflower, some explanation is needed, to wit, that Chiron, the fabulous centaur, was said to have employed these herbs in the exercise of his healing art.

The commemorative names are mostly given in honour of accomplished botanists, it being a habit of mankind, presumably prompted by the acquisitive instincts of the race, to name any object, great or small—from a mountain to a mouse—as*belonging* to the person who discovered or brought it to notice. In the case of wildflowers this is not always a very felicitous system of distinguishing them, though perhaps better than the utilitarian jargon of the pharmacopœia. Sometimes, indeed, it is beyond cavil; as in the fit association of the little *linnæa borealis* with the great botanist who loved it; but when a number of the less important professors of the science are immortalized in this way, there seems to be something rather irrelevant, if not absurd, in such nomenclature. Why, for example, should two of the more charming crucifers be named respectively *Hutchinsia* and *Teesdalia*, after a Miss Hutchins and a Mr. Teesdale? Why should the water-primrose be called *Hottonia*, after a Professor Hotton; or the sea-heath *Frankenia*, after a Swedish botanist named Franken; and so on, in a score of other cases that might be cited? The climax is reached when the *rubi* and the *salices* are divided into a host of more or less dubious sub-species, so that a Bloxam may have his bramble, and a Hoffmann his willow, as a possession for all time!

The most rational, and also the most graceful manner of naming flowers is the descriptive; and here, luckily, there are a number of titles, English or Latin, with which no fault can be found. Spearwort, mouse-tail, arrow-head, bird's-foot, colt's-foot, blue-bell, bindweed, crane's-bill, snapdragon, shepherd's purse, skull-cap, monk's-hood, ox-tongue—these are but a few of the well-bestowed names which, by an immediate appeal to the eye, fix the flower in the mind; they are at once simple and appropriate: in others, such as Adonis, Columbine, penny-cress, cranberry, lady's-mantle, and thorow-wax, the description, if less manifest at first sight, is none the less charming when recognized. The Latin, too, is at times so befitting as to be accepted without demur; thus *iris*, to express the rainbow tints of the flowers, needs no English equivalent, and *campanula* has only to be literally rendered as "bell-flower." In *campanula hederacea*, the "ivy-leaved bell-flower," we see nomenclature at its best, the petals and the foliage of a floral gem being both faithfully described.

A glance at a list of British wildflowers will bring to mind various other ways in which names have been given to them—some familiar, some romantic, a few even poetical. Among the homely but not unpleasing kind, are "Jack by the hedge" for the garlic mustard; "John go to bed at noon" for the goat's-beard; "creeping Jenny" for the money-wort; and "lady's-fingers" for the kidney-vetch. Of the romantically named plants the most conspicuous example is doubtless the forget-me-not, its English name contrasting, as it does, with the more realistic Latin *myosotis*, which detects in the shape of the leaves a likeness to a mouse's ear. None, perhaps, can claim to be so poetical as Gerarde's name for the clematis; for "traveller's joy" was one of those happy inspirations which are unfortunately rare.

# VI
## THE OPEN DOWNLAND

WHEN speaking of some Sussex water-meadows, I mentioned as one of their many delights the views which they offer of the never distant Downs. The charm of these chalk hills is to me only inferior to that of real mountains; there are times, indeed, when with clouds resting on the summits, or drifting slowly along the coombes, one could almost imagine himself to be in the true mountain presence. I have watched, on an autumn day, a long sea of vapour rolling up from the weald against the steep northern front of the Downs, while their southern slopes were still basking in sunshine; and scarcely less wonderful than the clouds themselves are the cloud-shadows that may often be seen chasing each other across the wide open tracts which lie in the recesses of the hills.

"Majestic mountains," "exalted promontories," were among the descriptions given of the Downs by Gilbert White: what we now prize in them is not altitude but spaciousness. In Rosamund Marriott Watson's words:

Broad and bare to the skies
The great Down-country lies.

Its openness, with the symmetry of the free curves and contours into which the chalk shapes itself, is the salient feature of the range; and to this may be added its liberal gift of solitude and seclusion. Even from the babel of Brighton an hour's journey on foot can bring one into regions where a perpetual Armistice Day is being celebrated, with something better than the two minutes of silence snatched from the townsfolk's day of din.

The Downs are also open in the sense of being free, to a very great extent, from the enclosures which in so many districts exclude the public from the land. In some parts, unfortunately, the abominable practice of erecting wire fences is on the increase among sheep-farmers; but generally speaking, a naturalist may here wander where he will.

Of all the flowering plants of the Downs, the gorse is at once the earliest and the most impressive; no spectacle that English wildflowers can offer, when seen *en masse*, excels that of the numberless furze-bushes on a bright April day. There is then a vividness in the gorse, a depth and warmth of that "deep gold colour" beloved by Rossetti, which far surpasses the glazed metallic sheen of a field of buttercups. It is pure gold, in bullion, the palpable wealth of Crœsus, displayed not in flat surfaces, but in bars, ingots, and spires, bough behind bough, distance on distance, with infinite variety of light and shade, and set in strong relief against a background of sombre foliage. Thus it has the appearance, in full sunshine, almost of a furnace, a reddish underglow and heart of flame which is lacking even in the broom. To creep within one of these gorse-temples when illumined by the sun, is to enjoy an ecstasy both of colour and of scent.

With the exception of the furze, the Downland flowers are mostly low of stature, as befits their exposed situation, a small but free people inhabiting the wind-swept slopes and coombes, and well requiting the friendship of those who visit them in their fastnesses. One of the earliest and most welcome is the spring whitlow-grass, which abounds on ant-

40

hills high up on the ridges, forming a dense growth like soft down on the earth's cheek. Here it hastes to get its blossoming done before the rush of other plants, its little reddish stalk rising from a rosette of short leaves, and bearing the tiny terminal flowers with white deeply cleft petals and anthers of yellow hue. Its near successor is the equally diminutive mouse-ear (*cerastium semidecandrum*), a white-petalled plant of a deep dark green, viscous, and thickly covered with hairs.

When summer has come, the flowers of the Downs are legion—yellow bird's-foot trefoil, and horse-shoe vetch; milkwort pink, white, or blue; fragile rock-rose; graceful dropwort; salad burnet; squinancy-wort, and a hundred more, of which one of the fairest, though commonest, is the trailing silverweed, whose golden petals are in perfect contrast with the frosted silver of the foliage. But the special ornament of these hills, known as "the pride of Sussex," is the round-headed rampion, a small, erect, blue-bonneted flower which is no "roundhead" in the Puritan sense, but rather of the gay company of cavaliers. Abundant along the Downs from Eastbourne to Brighton, and still further to the west, it is a plant of which the eye never tires.

But it is the orchids that chiefly draw one's thoughts to Downland when midsummer is approaching. "Have you seen the bee orchis?" is then the question that is asked; and to wander on the lower slopes at that season without seeing the bee orchis would argue a tendency to absent-mindedness. I used to debate with myself whether the likeness to a bee is real or fanciful, till one day, not thinking of orchids at all, I stopped to examine a rather strange-looking bee which I noticed on the grass, and found that the insect was—a

41

flower. That, so far, settled the point; but I still think that the fly orchis is the better imitation of the two.

The early spider orchis is native on the eastern range of the Downs, near the lonely hamlet of Telscombe and in a few other localities in the heart of the hills; where, unless one has luck—and I had none—the search for a small flower on those far-stretching slopes is like the proverbial hunt for a needle in a hayloft. The only noticeable object on the hillside was an apparently dead sheep, about a hundred feet below me, lying flat on her back, with hoofs pointing rigidly to the sky; but as it was *orchis*, not *ovis*, that I was in quest of, I was about to pass on, when I saw a shepherd, who had just come round a shoulder of the Down, uplift the sheep and set her on her legs, whereupon, to my surprise, she ambled away as if nothing had been amiss with her. I learnt from the shepherd that such accidents are not uncommon, and that having once "turned turtle" the sluggish creature (as mankind has made her) would certainly have perished unless he had chanced to come to the rescue. When I told the good man what had brought me to that unfrequented coombe, he said, as country people often do, that he did not "take much notice" of wildflowers; nevertheless, after inquiring about the appearance of the orchids, he volunteered to note the place for me if he chanced to see them. Then, as we were parting, he called after me: "And if you see any more sheep on their backs, I'll thank you if you'll turn 'em over." This I willingly promised, on the principle not only of humanity, but that one good turn deserves another. Next season, perhaps, our friendly compact may be renewed.

The dingle in which Telscombe lies is rich in flowers; in the Maytime of which I am speaking, there was a profusion of hound's-tongue in bloom, and a good sprinkling of that

42

charming upland plant, deserving of a pleasanter name, the field fleawort; but of what I was searching for, no trace. I had walked into the spider's "parlour," but the spider was not at home. More fortunate was a lady who on that same day brought to the Hove exhibition a flower which she had casually picked on another part of the Downs where she was taking a walk. Sitting down for a rest, she saw an unknown plant on the turf. It was a spider orchis.

Much less unaccommodating, to me, was the musk orchis, a still smaller species which grows in several places where the northern face of the Downs is intersected, as below Ditchling Beacon, by deep-cut tracks—they can hardly be called bridle-paths—that slant upward across the slope. I was told by Miss Robinson, of Saddlescombe, to whose wide knowledge of Sussex plants many flower-lovers besides myself have been indebted, that she once picked a musk orchis from horseback as she was riding along the hill side. It is a sober-garbed little flower, with not much except its rarity to signalize it; but an orchis is an orchis still; there is no member of the family that has not an interest of its own. Many of them are locally common on these hills; to wit, the early purple, the fly, the frog, the fragrant, the spotted, the pyramidal, and most lovely of all, the dwarf orchis; also the twayblade, the lady's-tresses, and one or two of the helleborines. The green-man orchis, not uncommon in parts of Surrey and Kent, will here be sought in vain.

But the Downs are not wholly composed of grassy sheep-walks and furze-dotted wastes; they include many tracts of cultivated land, where, if we may judge from the botanical records of the past generation, certain cornfield weeds which are now very rare, such as the mouse-tail and the hare's-ear, were once much more frequent. It is rather strange that the improved culture, which has nearly eliminated several interesting species, should have had so little effect on the charlock and the poppy, which still colour great squares and sections of the Downs with their rival tints, their yellow and scarlet rendered more conspicuous by having the quiet tones of these rolling uplands for a background.

In autumn, when most of the wealden flowers are withering, the chalk hills are still decked with gentians and other late-growing kinds; and the persistence, even into sere October, of such children of the sun as the rampion and the rock-rose is very remarkable. The autumnal aspect of the Downs is indeed as beautiful as any; for there are then many days when a blissful calm seems to brood over the great coombes and hollows, and the fields lie stretched out like a many-coloured map, the rich browns of the ploughlands splashed and variegated with patches of yellow and green. Then, too, one sees and hears overhead the joy-flight of the rooks and daws, as round and round they circle, higher and higher, like an inverted maelstrom swirling upward, till it breaks with a chorus of exulting cries as gladdening to the ear as is the sight of those aerial manœuvres to the eye.

The final impression which the Downs leave on the mind is, I repeat, one of freedom and space; and this is felt by the flower-lover as strongly as by any wanderer on these hills, these "blossoming places in the wilderness," as Mr. Hudson has called them, "which make the thought of our trim, pretty, artificial gardens a weariness."

# VII
## PRISONERS OF THE PARTERRE

THE domestication of plants, as of animals, is a concern of such practical importance that in most minds it quite transcends whatever interest may be felt in the beauty of wildflowers. But the many delights of the garden ought not to blind us to the fact that there is in the wild a peculiar quality which the domesticated can never reproduce, and that the plant which is free, even if it be the humblest and most common, has a charm for the nature-lover which the more gorgeous captives of the garden must inevitably lack. If much is gained by domestication, much is also lost. This, doubtless, is felt less strongly in the taming of plants than of animals, but in either case it holds true.

To some of us, it must be owned, zoological gardens are a nightmare of confusion, and the now almost equally popular "rock-garden" a place which leaves an impression of dullness and futility; for while we fully recognize the interest, such as it is, of inducing Alpines to grow under altered conditions of climate, there is an irrelevance in the assembling of heterogeneous flowers in one enclosure, which perplexes and wearies the mind. For just as a cosmopolitan city is no city at all, and a Babel is no language, so a multifarious rock-garden, where a host of alien plants are grouped in unnatural juxtaposition, is a collection not of flowers but of "specimens." For scientific purposes—the determination of species, and viewing the plants in all stages of their growth—it may be most valuable: to the mere flower-lover, as he gazes on such a concourse, the thought that arises is: "What's Hecuba to him, or he to Hecuba?" It is a museum, a herbarium, if you like; but hardly, in any true sense, a garden.

I once had the experience of living next door to a friend who was smitten with the mania for rock-gardening, and from my study window I overlooked the process from start to finish—first the arrival of many tons of limestone blocks and chips; then the construction of artificial crags and gullies, moraines and escarpments, until a line of miniature Alps rose to view; and lastly the planting of various mountain flowers in the situations suited to their needs. Then followed many earnest colloquies between the creator of this fair scene and a neighbour enthusiast, as they walked about the garden together and inspected it plant by plant, much as a farmer goes his rounds to examine his oats or turnips. They surveyed the world, botanically speaking, from China to Peru. Yet somehow I felt that, just as I would rather see a sparrow at large than an eagle in captivity, so to be shown round that well-fashioned rockery was less entertaining than to show oneself round the most barren of the adjacent moors. "Herbes that growe in the fieldes," wrote a fifteenth-century herbalist, "be bettere than those that growe in gardenes."

This, however, is by no means the common opinion; on the contrary, there is in most minds a disregard or veritable contempt for wildflowers as being, with a few exceptions, "weeds," and quite unworthy of comparison with the inmates of a garden.

In her *Haunts of the Wild Flowers*, Anne Pratt has recorded how she was invited by a cottager to throw away a bunch of "ordinary gays" that she was carrying, and to gather some garden flowers in their stead.

I once took a long walk over the moors in Derbyshire in order to visit certain rare flowers of the limestone dales, among them the speedwell-leaved whitlow-grass (*draba muralis*), a specimen of which I brought home. This little crucifer is very insignificant in appearance; and the fact that anyone should plod many miles to gather it so upset the gravity of an extremely demure and respectful servant girl, when she saw it on my mantelpiece, that to her own visible shame and confusion she broke into a loud giggle, somewhat as Bernard Shaw's chocolate-cream soldier failed to conceal his amusement when the portrait of the hero of the cavalry charge was shown to him by its possessor.

Even in the case of those wildings whose beauty or scent has made them generally popular, it is thought the highest compliment to domesticate them, to bring them—poor waifs and strays that they are—from their forlorn savage state into the fold of civilization, just as a "deserving" pauper might be received into an almshouse, or an orphan child into one of Dr. Barnardo's homes. And strange to say, this reverential belief in the garden, as enhancing the merits of the wild, has found its way into many of the wildflower books: for instance, in Johns's well-known work, *Flowers of the Field* (of the *field*, be it noted), we are informed that the lily of the valley is "a universally admired garden plant, and that the sweet-brier is "deservedly" cultivated.

The more refined wildflowers, it will be seen, can thus rise, as it were, from the ranks, at the cost of their freedom, which happens to be the most interesting thing about them, to be enrolled in the army of the civilized; and the result has been that some of the more distinguished plants, such as the *daphne mezereum*, are fast losing their place among British wildflowers, and becoming nothing better than prisoners and captives of the parterre. This disdain that is felt for whatever is wild, natural, and unowned, is largely responsible for the unscrupulous digging up of any attractive plants that may be discovered, a subject of which I propose to speak in the next chapter.

The absurdity of the typical gardener's attitude toward wildflowers is well illustrated by some remarks in Delamer's *The Flower Garden* (1856) with reference to that exceedingly beautiful plant, the tutsan. "Tutsan is a hardy shrubby St. John's-wort, largely employed by gardeners of the last century; but it has now, for the most part, retired from business, in consequence of the arrival of more attractive and equally serviceable newcomers. One or two tutsan bushes may be permitted to help to form a screen of shrubs, in consideration of the days of auld lang syne."

Fortunately the tutsan is not "retiring from business" in Nature's garden. It seems to me that, instead of carrying more and more wildflowers into captivity, it would be much wiser to set at liberty the many British plants that are now under detention. I would instruct my gardener (if I had one) to lift very carefully the daphnes, the lilies of the valley, the tutsans, the cornflowers, the woodruffs, and the rest of the native clan, and to plant them out, each according to its taste, by bank or hedgerow, in field, common, or wood.

# VIII
## PICKING AND STEALING

THERE is, as I have said, a positive contempt in many minds for the wildflower; that is, for the flower which is regarded as being no one's "property." But the flora of a country, rightly considered, is very far from being unowned; it is the property of the people, and when any species is diminished or extirpated the loss is not private but national. We have already reached a time, as many botanists think, when the choicer British flowers need some sort of protection.

That some injury should be caused to our native flora by improved culture, drainage, building, and the extension of towns, is inevitable; though these losses might be considerably lessened if there were a more general regard for natural beauty. But that is all the stronger reason for discountenancing such damage as is done in mere thoughtlessness, or, worse, for selfish purposes; and it were greatly to be wished that some of the good folk who pray that their hands may be kept "from picking and stealing" would so far widen the scope of their sympathies as to include the rarer wildflowers.

It cannot be doubted that there is an immense amount of wasteful flower-picking by children, and also by persons who are old enough to know better. Nothing is commoner, in Spring, than to see piles of freshly gathered hyacinths or cowslips abandoned by the roadside; and many other flowers share the same fate, including, as I have noticed, the beautiful green-winged meadow orchis. Trippers and holiday-makers are often very mischievous: I have seen them, for instance, on the ramparts of Conway Castle, hooking and tearing the red valerian which is an ornament to the grey old walls. I was told by a friend who lives in a district where the rare meadow-sage (*salvia pratensis*) is native, that he is compelled to pluck the blue flowers just before the August bank-holiday, in order to save the plant itself from being up-rooted and carried off.

Primroses, abundant as they still are in many places, have nearly disappeared from others, in consequence of the depredations of flower-vendors; and there was a time when they were seriously threatened in the neighbourhood of London because a certain fashionable cult was at its height.

The nurseryman and the professional gardener have also much to answer for in the destruction of wildflowers. Take the following instance, quoted from the *Flora of Kent*, with reference to the cyclamen: "Towards the end of August, 1861, I was shown the native station of this plant. . . . The people in those parts had found out it was in request, and had almost entirely extirpated it, digging up the roots, and selling them for transplantation into shrubberies." In the same work it is recorded that, when the frog orchis was found in some abundance near Canterbury, "in a wonderfully short space of time the whole of this charming colony was dug and extirpated."

Again, if it be permissible to call a spade a spade, what shall be said of those roving knights of the trowel, the unconscionable rock-gardeners who ride abroad in search of some new specimen for their collections? A late writer of very charming books on the subject has feelingly described how, after the discovery of some long-sought treasure, he craved a brief spell of repose, a sort of holy calm, before commencing operations. "We blessed ones," he said, referring to botanists as contrasted with ornithologists, "may sit down calmly, philosophically, beside our success, and gently savour all its sweetness, until it is time to take out the trowel after half an hour of restful rapture in our laurels."

Other flower-fanciers there are who show much less circumspection. In Upper Teesdale, where the rare blue gentian (*gentiana verna*) is found on the upland pastures, I was told that a "gentleman" had come with two gardeners in a motor, and departed laden with a number of these beautiful Alpine flowers for transplantation to his private rockery. The nation which permits such a theft—far worse than stealing from a private garden—deserves to possess no wildflowers at all; and such a botanist, if botanist he can be called, deserves to be himself transplanted, or transported—to Botany Bay.

The same vandalism, in varying degrees, has been at work in every part of the land, and nothing has yet been done effectively to check it, whether by legislation, education, or appeal to public opinion: it seems to be absolutely no one's business to protect what ought to be a cherished national possession. In no district, perhaps, has the greed of the collector been more unabashed than among the mountains of Cumberland and North Wales. "Thanks to the inconsiderate rapacity of the fern-getter," wrote Canon Rawnsley, in an Introduction to a *Guide to Lakeland*, "the few rarer sorts are fast disappearing. ... There has been, in the time past, quite a cruel and unnecessary uprooting of the rarer ferns and flowers;" and he went on to ask: "When will travellers learn that the fern by the wayside has a public duty to fulfil?"

All such remonstrances have hitherto been in vain: neither the fear of God nor the fear of man has deterred the collector from his purpose. It is pleasant to read that in the seventeenth century a Welsh guide alleged "the fear of eagles" as a reason for not leading one of the earliest English visitors to the haunts of Alpine plants on the precipices of Carnedd Llewelyn; but unfortunately eagles are now as scarce as nurserymen and fern-filchers are numerous.

# IX
## ROUND A SURREY CHALK-PIT

As a range of hills, the North Downs are inferior to those of Sussex in beauty and general interest. Their outline suggests no "greyhound backs" coursing along the horizon; nor have they that "living garment" of turf, woven by centuries of pasturing, which Hudson has matchlessly described. Their northern side is but a gradual slope leading up to a bleak tableland; and only when one emerges suddenly on their southern front, with its wide views across the weald, do their glories begin to be realized. In this steep declivity, facing the sun at noon, there is a distinctive and unfailing charm, quite unlike that of the corresponding escarpment of the South Downs: it forms, as it were, an inland riviera, a sheltered undercliff, green with long waving grasses, and sweet with marjoram and thyme, a haven where the wandering flower-lover may revel in glowing sunshine, or take a siesta, if so minded, under that most friendly of trees the white-beam.

I have memories of many a pious Sabbath spent in this enchanted realm, with the wind in the beeches for anthem, and for incense the scent of marjoram enriching the air. To one who knows these fragrant banks it seems strange that though the wild thyme has been so celebrated by poets and nature-writers, the marjoram, itself a glorified thyme, has by comparison gone unsung. We are told in the books that it is a potherb, an aromatic stimulant, even a remedy for toothache. It may be all that; but it is something much better, a thing of beauty which might cure the achings not of the tooth only, but of the heart. Its relatives the lavender and the rosemary have not more charm. It was the *amaracus* of Virgil, the flower on whose sweetness the young Iulus rested, when he was spirited away by Venus to her secret abode:

She o'er the prince entrancing slumber strows,
And, fondling in her bosom, far away
Bears him aloft to high Idalian bowers,
Where banks of marjoram sweet, in soft repose,
Enfold him, propped on beds of fragrant flowers.
Who could wish for a diviner couch?

Along this range of hills the chalk-pits, used or disused, are frequent at intervals, some of such size as to form landmarks visible at the distance of twenty or thirty miles. For a botanist, these amphitheatres, large or small, have always an attraction; for though they vary much in the quality of their flowers, and some have little to show beyond the commoner plants of a calcareous soil, there are a few which present a surprising array of the choicer kinds; and to light upon one of these treasure-troves is a joy indeed. I have in mind a large semicircular disused pit, lying high among the Downs, and bordered with abrupt grassy banks and coppices of beech, hazel, and fir, where during the past thirty years I have spent many long summer days, sometimes writing under the shade of the trees, at other times idling among the flowers, or watching the snakes that lie basking in the sun, or the kestrels that may often be seen hovering over the adjacent slopes. For all their unrivalled openness and sense of space, the Sussex Downs have no such "sun-trap" to show.

One has heard of "the music of wild flowers." I used to call the floor of this chalk-pit "the orchistra," so numerous are the orchids that adorn it. The spotted orchis, the fragrant orchis, the pyramidal orchis, the bee orchis, the butterfly orchis, and the twayblade—these six are stationed there within a small compass. The marsh orchis grows below; the fly orchis is in the neighbouring thickets; in the beech-woods are the bird's-nest orchis, the broad-leaved helleborine, with its rare purple variety (*epipactis purpurata*), and the large white helleborine or egg orchis. A dozen of the family within the circuit of a short walk! The man orchis seems to be absent, though it grows in some plenty in similar places on the same line of hills.

Another feature of the chalk-pit is the viper's bugloss. If, as Thoreau says, there is a flower for every mood of the mind, the viper's bugloss must surely belong to that mood which is associated with the pomps and splendours of the high summer noontide. Gorgeous and tropical in its colouring beyond all other British flowers, as it rears its bristly green spikes, studded profusely with the pink buds that are turning to an equally vivid blue, it seems instinct with the spirit of a fiery summer day. Like other members of the Borage group, it has the warm southern temperament; its name, too, suits it well; for there is something viperish in the almost fierce beauty of the plant, as if some passionate-hearted exotic had sprung up among the more staid and sober representatives of our native flora. Its richness never palls on us; we no more tire of its brilliance than of the summer itself.

Akin to the bugloss, though less striking and less abundant, is the hound's-tongue, with its long downy leaves and numerous purple-red buds of a sombre and sullen hue that is not often to be matched. It has the misfortune, so we are told, to smell of mice; were it not for this hindrance to its career, it might justly be held in high esteem. Among the larger plants prominent on ledges of the chalk, or in near neighbourhood, are the mullein, the teazle, the ploughman's-spikenard, and the deadly nightshade. The buckthorn is frequent in the hedges and thickets; and the traveller's-joy is climbing wherever it can get a hold.

But it is on the shelving banks that skirt the margin of the pit that the comeliest flowers are to be found; the most beautiful of all, perhaps, is the rock-rose, a plant so delicate that its small golden petals will scarcely survive a journey in the vasculum, yet so hardy that it will flower to the very latest autumn days. The wild strawberry is creeping everywhere; and the crimson of the grass vetchling may occasionally be seen among the ranker herbage, to which the stalk seems to belong; on the shorter turf is the small squinancy-wort, lovely cousin of the woodruff, its pink and white petals chiselled like the finest ivory.

The elegant yellow-wort, glaucous and perfoliate, and the handsome pink centaury, are common on the Downs; so, too, in the late summer, will be their less showy but always welcome relative, the autumnal gentian: all three have the firm and erect habit that is a property of the Gentian tribe. It is one of the many merits of these chalk hills that their flower-season is a prolonged one. Not the gentians only, with yellow-wort and centaury, are still vigorous in the autumn, but also the blue fleabane, clustered bell-flower, vervain, marjoram, basil, and many labiate herbs. Even in October, when the glory has long departed from the lowlands of the weald, there remains a brave show of blossom on these delectable hills.

The Pilgrim's Way, often no more than a grassy track, runs eastward along the base of the Downs, interrupted here and there by the encroachment of parks and private estates, which now block the ancient route to Canterbury; but where

Nature has provided so many shrines and cathedrals of her own, there is no need of any others; certainly I never lacked a holy place wherein to make my vows, many as were the pilgrimages on which I started.

On one occasion that I recall, I was joined in my quest by a rather strange fellow-traveller, a man who met me, coming from the opposite direction, and eagerly asked whether I had seen anyone on the hillside. When I assured him that nobody had passed that way, he turned and walked in my company, and presently confided to me that he was an attendant at a lunatic asylum, and was in pursuit of an inmate who had escaped an hour or two before. We went a short distance together, he peering into the coombes and bushy hollows, as incongruous a pair as could be imagined; yet it occurred to me that his mission, too, might be considered a botanical one, since there is a plant named the madwort— nay, worse, the "German madwort," a title which, in those feverish war-days, would of itself have justified incarceration. Nevertheless, as I always sympathize with escaped prisoners (provided, of course, that it is not *my* bed under which they conceal themselves), I was secretly glad that my companion's search was unavailing.

To return to my chalk-pit: I have mentioned but a few of the many flowers that belong there; within a mile, or less, others and quite different ones are flourishing. The rampion, though very local in Surrey, is found in places along these Downs; so, too, is the strange yellow bugle, or "ground pine," which is much more like a diminutive pine than a bugle; also the still stranger fir-rape (*monotropa*), which lurks in the thickest shade of the beech-woods. That interesting shrub, the butcher's-broom, or "knee holly," as it is more agreeably called, is another native: it wears its small flower daintily, like a button-hole, on the centre of the rigid leaves of deepest green.

A few miles east there is another chalk-pit which, though inferior in the number of its flowers, has a sprinkling of the man orchis, whose shape, if there is any likeness at all, seems to suggest a toy man dangling from a string; a simile which I prefer to that of a dead man dangling from the gallows. In the woods that crown this pit there is a profusion of the deadly nightshade; and I noticed that during the war-summers, when there was a scarcity of belladonna, these plants were regularly harvested by some enterprising herbalist.

Such are a few of the delights of the Surrey undercliff; but alas! they are vanishing delights, for the proximity to London has rendered all this district peculiarly liable to change. How could it be otherwise, when from the top of the ridge the dome of "smoky Paul's" is visible on a clear day, and a view of the Crystal Palace, "that dreadful C.P." as one has heard it called, can seldom be avoided. What havoc has been wrought in the Surrey hills by the advance of "civilization," may be learnt by anyone who studies the district with a sixty-year-old *Flora of Surrey* for guide. Between Merstham and Godstone, for instance, the hillsides, which were then free, open ground, have become in the saddest sense "residential," and the wildflowers have suffered in proportion. One may still find there the narrow-leaved everlasting pea, "hanging in festoons on thickets and copses," but other equally valued plants have disappeared or are disappearing. The marsh helleborine was once plentiful, it seems, in a swampy situation near Merstham; but when, by dint of careful trespassing and circumnavigation of barbed wire, I reached a place which corresponded exactly with that indicated in the *Flora*, not a single flower was to be seen. Probably some conscientious gardener had "transplanted" them.

It is impossible to doubt that this process will be continued, and that every year more wild land will be broken up in the building of villas and in the making of gardens, with the inevitable shrubberies, gravel walks, flower-borders, and lawn-tennis courts. The trim parterre with its "detested calceolarias," as a great nature-lover has described them, will more and more be substituted for the rough banks that are the favourite haunts of marjoram and rock-rose. How can the owners of such a fairyland have the heart to sell it for such a purpose? In Omar's words:

I often wonder what the vintners buy
One half so precious as the stuff they sell.

# XI
## QUAINTNESS IN FLOWERS

I SPOKE just now of a love of the quaint. Quaintness, though it may exist apart from beauty, is often associated with it, and, unlike grotesqueness, has a pleasurable interest for the spectator. In flowers it is usually suggested by some abnormality of shape, as in the snapdragon; less frequently, as in the fritillary, by a singular effect of colouring. Perhaps it is to the orchis group that one would most confidently apply the word; for they arrest attention not so much by their beauty as by their strangeness: one of them, indeed, the dwarf orchis, is undeniably beautiful, while another, the bird's-nest, is as ugly as a broom-rape; the others, if one tried to find a comprehensive epithet, might fairly be described as quaint.

This quality in the orchids is not due solely to the odd likeness which some of them present to certain insects; for, as far as British species are concerned, the similarity, with a few exceptions, is somewhat fanciful. If it be granted that the fly, the bee, and the spider orchis are justly named—though even in these the resemblance is not always recognized when pointed out—it is no less true that one looks in vain for the semblance of a "butterfly," or of a "frog," in the plants that are so entitled, and it takes some ingenuity to discover the "man" in *aceras anthropophora*, or the "egg" in the white helleborine. But there is a charming quaintness in nearly all members of the family, owing largely to the peculiar structure of the lower lip of the corolla or the unusual length of the spur.

The very name of the snapdragon is a proof of its hold upon the imagination: what mediæval romance and unfailing charm for children—and for adults—is conveyed in the word! The plant is at its best when clad in royal hue of purple; the white robe also has its glory; but the intermediate forms, striped and mottled, that are so fancied in gardens, are degenerates from a noble type. Seen on the walls of some ancient ruin, the snapdragon is a wonder and a delight; it is to be regretted that its place is now so often usurped by the red valerian, in comparison a mere upstart and pretender. The lesser snapdragon or calf's-snout, with the toadflaxes and fluellens, shares in the characteristic quaintness of its tribe.

I will next instance the "perfoliates," plants not confined to any one order, but alike in having a stem which passes midway through the leaf or pair of leaves, a most engaging curiosity of structure. It is by this peculiarity that the yellow-wort, a gentian with glaucous foliage and blossoms like "patines of bright gold," mainly wins its popularity. But the quaintest of perfoliates is the hare's-ear, or "thorow-wax," as it used to be called, of which, as Gerarde wrote, "every branch grows thorow every leaf, making them like hollow cups or saucers." The thorow-wax owes its attractiveness to these singular glaucous leaves, which might be compared with an artist's palette; in some measure, also, to the sharp-pointed bracts by which the minute yellow flowers are enfolded—features that lend it a distinction which many much more beautiful plants do not possess.

From no catalogue of quaint plants could the butterwort be omitted. "Mountain-sanicle" was its old name; and all climbers are acquainted with it, as it studs the wet rocks on the lower hillsides with pale green or yellowish leaves like starfish on a seashore. Its flowering-season is short, but full of interest, for lo! from its centre there rise in June one or two long and dainty stems, each bearing at its extremity a drooping purple flower that might at first glance be taken for a violet—a violet springing from a starfish!

It is a long step from these conspicuous examples of the quaint to the small and modest moschatel, a hedge-flower which is likely to go unobserved unless it be made a special object of inquiry. *Adoxa*, "the unknown to fame," is its Greek title; but if it has little claim to beauty in the ordinary sense, there is no slight charm in its delicate configuration, and in the whimsical arrangement of its five slender flower-heads— a terminal one, facing upwards, supported by four lateral ones, with a resemblance to the faces of a clock; whence it's not inappropriate nickname, "the clock-tower." A fairy-like little belfry it is, whose chimes must be listened for, if at all, in the early spring, for it hastens to get its flowering finished before it is overgrown by the rank herbage of the roadside.

There are many other flowers that might claim a place in this chapter, such as the sundews and the bladderworts; the mimulus and ground pine; the samphire and sea-rocket; the mullein and the teazle; and not least, the herb Paris, with that large quadruple "love-knot" into which its leaves are fashioned. But it must suffice to speak of one more.

The fritillary, which shall close the list, is quaint to the point of being bizarre: its various names bear witness to the freakishness of its apparel—"guinea-flower," "turkey-hen," "chequered lily," "snake's-head," and so forth. It was aptly described by Gerarde as "chequered most strangely. . . . Surpassing the curiousest painting that art can set down"; and in addition to this gorgeous colouring, the bell-like shape and heavy poise of its flower-heads contribute to the striking effect. From Gerarde to W. H. Hudson, who has portrayed it very beautifully in his *Book of a Naturalist*, the fritillary has been fortunate in its chroniclers; in its name, which it shares with a handsome family of butterflies, it can hardly be said to have been fortunate. For apart from the consideration that it is no great honour to a fine insect or flower to be likened to that instrument of human folly, a dicebox (*fritillus*), there is the practical difficulty of pronouncing the word as the dictionaries tell us it must be pronounced, with the accent on the first syllable; and not the dictionaries only, but the poets, as in Arnold's oft-quoted but very cacophonous line:

I know what white, what purple fritillaries. . . .

Why must so quaintly charming a flower be so barbarously named that one's jaw is well-nigh cracked in articulating it?

# XII
## HERTFORDSHIRE CORNFIELDS

THAT part of Hertfordshire where the Chiltern Hills, after curving proudly round from Tring to Dunstable, and almost rivalling the South Downs in shapeliness, die away at their north-east extremity, over Hitchin, to a bare expanse of ploughland, has the aspect of a broad plain swept by all winds of heaven, but is found, when explored, to be by no means devoid of charm. There, by a paradox, the very extent of the great hedgeless cornfields, reclaimed from the wild, gives the landscape a sort of wildness; it is in fact the district whence the Royston crow got its name, that hooded outlaw to whose survival a wide tract of open country was indispensable; and there is a pleasure in wandering over it which is unguessed by the traveller who rushes through in an express to Cambridge, and marvels at the tameness of the land.

The wildflowers of cultivated fields are as distinctive as those of heath or hillside. It would be difficult to name any two more beautiful "weeds" than the succory and the corn "blue-bottle"—the light blue and the dark blue; both have deservedly won their "blues"—and when to these is added the corn-cockle (*lychnis githago*), the rich veined purple of its petals set off by the long pointed green sepals and leaves, what handsomer trio could be wished? Unhappily these flowers have become much scarcer than they used to be; but in the Hertfordshire fields they are still frequently to be admired.

The intensive culture of which we nowadays hear so much has this drawback for the botanist, that it is robbing him of some plants which he is very loth to lose. The most striking of these, perhaps, is that quaint "perfoliate" of which I have already spoken, the thorow-wax or hare's-ear, which in Gerarde's time was so plentiful in the wheatland as to be what he calls its "infirmitie": now it is decidedly rare. I have never been so fortunate (except in dreams) as to see it *in situ*; but I have for several years grown it from the seed of a specimen gathered by a friend in the cornfields near Baldock, and have always been impressed by its elegance. It is a delicate and fastidious plant, thriving only, as I have noticed, when the conditions are quite favourable: this may account for its steady diminution in many counties, while coarser and hardier weeds are legion.

A more abiding "infirmitie" of some Hertfordshire cornfields is the crow-garlic, a wild onion whose pink umbels often surmount the crop in hundreds. Wishing to learn their local name, I once asked a farm-hand at Letchworth what he called the flowers. After gazing at them sternly, he said to me: "They're *not* flowers. They're a disease." I suggested that whatever their demerits might be from the point of view of an agriculturist, they must, strictly speaking, be regarded as flowers: this he grudgingly conceded; but as if regretting to have made so large an admission, he called after me, as I left him: "They're a disease." His pertinacity on this point reminded me of the reaffirmations of Old Kaspar, in Southey's poem, "After Blenheim":"Nay, nay" ... quoth he, "It was a famous victory."

The crow-garlic, as it happens, is rather a pretty plant; and the opprobrious name "disease" might be much more suitably assigned to the tall broom-rape, an unwholesome-looking parasite which lives rapaciously at the expense of the great knapweed, and is occasionally met with in the district of which I am speaking.

An extremely local umbellifer, said to have been formerly so abundant about Baldock that pigs were turned out to fatten on its roots, is the bulbous caraway, which looks like a larger edition of the common earth-nut. None of the country-folk whom I questioned seemed to have any knowledge of its uses; from which it would appear that its virtues, like those of many once famous herbs, have been forgotten in these sceptical modern times. It is well, perhaps, that *carum bulbocastanum* should be saved from the pigs; for in that unlovely region its white umbels serve to lighten up the monotony of the waysides.

An unexpected discovery is always welcome. In a waste field, about a mile from Royston, I once found a tall branching plant with an abundance of yellow cruciferous flowers, which I should not have recognized but for the fact that a year or two previously my friend Edward Carpenter had sent me a specimen from Corsica. It was the woad, famous as the source of the blue dye with which the ancient Britons stained themselves. A mere "casual" in Hertfordshire, it is said to be established in a few chalk-quarries near Guildford and elsewhere.

Thus far I have spoken of none but field flowers; but the district does not consist wholly of cultivated land, for even in that wilderness of tillage there are oases which have never felt the plough, and where the flora is of a different order. Therfield Heath, near Royston, is one of them, a grassy slope where the handsome purple milk-vetch is plentiful, and one may find, though in less abundance, the sprightly field fleawort, which seems more familiar as an ornament of the high chalk Downs.

Nor are water springs wanting in the bare ploughlands. The little river Ivel, which leaps suddenly[Pg 94] to light near Baldock, and thence races northward to join the Bedfordshire Ouse, is a clear trout-stream by whose banks it is pleasant (whatever the trespass notices may threaten) to wander, and to watch the quick-glancing fish. At the hamlet of Radwell, in a moist copse, there is a patch of the rare monk's-hood, a poisonous flower of which later mention will be made. A joint tributary of the Ouse, and not less inviting, is the oddly named Hiz, which has its source on Oughton Common, a boggy flat near Hitchin, where both the butterwort and the grass of Parnassus are recorded as having grown and may perchance be growing still: as for the marsh orchis, one cannot cross the Common without seeing it.

Then at Ickleford, a village on the banks of the Hiz, there is a pond which has been "occupied" (to use a military term) by the water-soldier, a stout aquatic which takes its name from the rigid swordlike leaves enclosing the three-petalled flowers. Peculiar to the eastern counties, this water-soldier is said to have been introduced at Ickleford over half a century ago; and there it now makes a fine array, having thriven wonderfully in spite of the worn-out pots and pans, and other refuse, for which, in Hertfordshire as elsewhere, the nearest pool or stream is thought a fit receptacle.

A mile or two west of the source of the Hiz at Oughton Head, stands High Down, where begins or ends, according to the direction of the wayfarer, the northern escarpment of the Chilterns, at this point crossed, recrossed, and crossed again, by the curiously indented boundary-line between Hertfordshire and Bedfordshire; and here on the steep front of the Pirton and Barton hills, in the one county or the other, may be seen in early spring the most beautiful of English anemones, the pasque-flower. On the few occasions when I have visited the place the summer was well advanced, and I was too late for that gorgeous flower; I had to content myself with the pyramidal orchis at the foot of the hills, and with great blossoming sheets of white candytuft in the fields above.

For all these excursions there is no better starting-point than Letchworth, first of Garden Cities, which has sprung rapidly into being from what was until recent years an unadorned expanse of agricultural ground with Norton Common as its centre. This Common, originally a bit of wild fen, now almost surrounded by cottages and gardens, is to the nature-lover the most attractive feature of Letchworth; and though its flora has inevitably suffered from the inroads of the juvenile population, it can still show such plants as the marsh orchis, the small valerian, and the rare sulphur-coloured trefoil. It is watered by a diminutive river—the unceremonious might say ditch—known as the Pix, whose current, like that of the Cam, would almost seem to be determined by the direction of the wind, but is reputed to flow northward, to join its fleeter brethren, the Hiz and the Ivel, in their course to the Ouse.

I mention this rather forlorn stream, because it has sometimes occurred to me that, as an attempt is made to protect the wild birds on Norton Common, it might be expedient to lend a helping hand also to the flowers, or even to embellish the banks of the Pix (and so to re-invite the pixies to sport thereby), with a few hardy riverside plants, such as comfrey, tansy, hemp-agrimony, purple loosestrife, and yellow loosestrife, which were probably once native there, and would almost certainly flourish in such a spot. Is it legitimate thus to come to the rescue of wild nature? That is a question on which botanists are not quite agreed, and its consideration shall therefore be reserved for the following chapter.

# XIII
## THE SOWER OF TARES

THE sowing of wildflowers is deprecated by some botanists, presumably as an interference with natural processes, an unauthorized attempt to play Providence in the vegetable kingdom; but the subject is one that seems to call for fuller discussion than it usually receives.

We are told in the parable that the man who sowed tares among the wheat was an enemy; and certainly if there was an intention to injure the crop the expression was not too strong. But I have sometimes wondered whether the reprehensible act may not have been that of some botanical enthusiast, who, loving wildflowers not wisely but too well, was trying to save from extinction some rare weed of the cornfields which was disappearing under improved methods of culture.

That this way of augmenting the flora of a country is nowadays not uncommon may be guessed from the frequent occurrence in botanical works of the comment "probably planted." Only a few pages back, I referred to the case of a pond in Hertfordshire now strongly held by a battalion of water-soldiers, the descendants of imported plants. There is evidence, too, that the practice has occasionally been indulged in by naturalists of great distinction, an amusing instance being that of the venerable and much-respected Gerarde, whose description of the peony as growing wild near Gravesend drew from his editor, Johnson, the following remark: "I have beene told that our author himselfe planted the peionie there, and afterwards seemed to finde it there by accident; and I doe believe it was so, because none before or since have ever seene or heard of it growing wilde in any part of this kingdome."

Again, it is stated in Canon Vaughan's *Wild Flowers of Selborne* that Gilbert White himself "was once guilty of this misdemeanour." He sowed, not tares in wheat, but seeds of the grass of Parnassus in the Hampshire bogs, and sowed them according to his own statement unsuccessfully; it would appear, however, from what Canon Vaughan discovered that White was "more successful than he imagined." However that may be, the question that arises is whether a judicious extension of the range of wildflowers by the agency of man is really a thing to be censured. May not a flower-lover occasionally sow his "wild oats"?

It must be admitted that the objections to such a practice are not retrospective, for if it be a misdemeanour, it is one that is condoned, perhaps hallowed, by time. For as it is impossible to draw a strict line between flowers that were accidentally imported or "escapes" from ancient gardens, and those that were planted deliberately, we wisely ask no questions in the case of old-established plants of foreign origin, but receive them into our flora as aliens that have become naturalized and are honourably classed as "denizens"; when they have once made good their tenure of the soil, it seems to matter little by what means they arrived. Thus, for example, the starry trefoil, which colonized the Shoreham shingles over a century ago, having apparently come as a stowaway on board some foreign ship, was not only tolerated but highly regarded by English botanists, and its recent destruction is felt to be a national loss. Would it have detracted from its value, if, as indeed may have happened, it had been purposely sown on the beach? On the contrary, it seems desirable that it should now be restored in that manner.

Such planting, of course, if done at all, should be done circumspectly, and on a fixed principle, not as an amusement for irresponsible persons or children. I know a flower-lover who, in a district where that beautiful St. John's-wort, the tutsan, was dwindling through depredations, or through some unexplained malady, carefully restored the balance in a score or so of suitable spots; and surely such action was much to be commended. But it is not desired that everyone should be planting tutsan everywhere; nor is there any danger of such a fashion arising, for there is much less tendency to plant than to pluck, to create than to destroy; and for that reason it would be folly to reintroduce any rare plant like the lady's slipper, where the collector would quickly reap what the enthusiast had sown.

Such was the objection, it seems to me, to a proposal made some years ago by Edward Carpenter and others, that the diminishing numbers of the rarer butterflies should be reinforced by breeding. One would not willingly repeat the comedy of the angling craze, which solemnly stocks rivers with fish in order to pull them out again for pastime.

Nor, because *some* planting of wildflowers may be unobjectionable, does it follow that all such enterprises are deserving of praise. A recent announcement that the Llanberis side of Snowdon, a locality rich in British mountain flowers, was being sown by Kew experts with the seeds of a number of "Alpines" from Switzerland, was likely to be more agreeable to rock-gardeners than to mountain-lovers, who have a regard for the distinctive character of Snowdon itself, and of its native flora. A country which has allowed its finest mountain to be exploited for commercial purposes, as Snowdon has been, is perhaps hardly in a position to protest against a Welsh hillside being planted with alien Swiss flowers, and even with Chinese rhododendrons; but nevertheless such schemes are thoroughly incongruous and barbaric. What sort of mountains do we desire to have? A piece of nature, or a nursery-garden? A Snowdon, or a Snowdon-cum-Kew?

Be it understood, then, that the sowing of tares is by no means recommended as a practice: all that is here urged is that a sweeping condemnation of it is not warranted by the facts, inasmuch as circumstances, not dogma, must in each case decide whether it be blameworthy, or harmless, or beneficial. And apart from common sense, there is one natural safeguard which will prevent any undue growth of wildflowers, viz. the remarkable fastidiousness of the choicer plants in regard to soil and conditions: they will flourish where it suits them to flourish, not elsewhere. Certain auxiliaries, too, Nature has in the rabbits, water-voles, and other wild animals that are herbivorous in their tastes; for it is very interesting to observe how quickly the appearance of a strange plant will attract the attention of such gourmands.

I was once the owner of a sloping meadow in which there were some springs; and thinking it would be pleasant to have a water-garden I had a small pond made, into which I introduced some aquatic plants, and among them, most accommodating of all, the water-violet, which grew lustily and sent up a number of its graceful stalks with whorls of pink blossoms. But just at that time a water-vole took up his residence there, and developing a remarkable fondness for a new savour in his salads, quickly made havoc of my

*Hottonia palustris*. The neighbours assured me I must trap him; but to treat a fellow-vegetarian in that way was out of the question, especially as his confidence in me was so great that he would sit nibbling my favourite aquatic, which seemed also to be *his* favourite, while I stood within a few yards. It was clear that if the cult of the water-violet involved the killing of the water-vole it had got to be abandoned.

In this way, among others, does Nature protect herself against an excessive interference on man's part with the distribution of wild flowers.

# XIV
## DALES OF DERBYSHIRE

THE limestone Dales of Derbyshire are narrow and deep, and their streams, when visible (for they often lurk underground), are swift, strong, and of crystal clearness. The sides of the glens are in some places precipitous with bluffs and pinnacles of grey rock; in others, ridged and streaked with terraces of alternate crag and turf; above the cliffs there is often a tableland of bleak pastures divided by stone walls, as dreary a scene as could be imagined, when contrasted with the picturesque dales below.

The flowers of these limestone valleys immediately recall those of the chalk: the marjoram, the basil, the great knapweed, the traveller's-joy, the rock-rose, the musk-thistle—these and many other familiar friends make us seem, at first sight, to be back in Sussex or Surrey. But in reality we are a hundred and fifty miles nearer to the arctic zone, and that difference is clearly reflected in the flora; for when we look around, a number of new plants make their appearance, of which a dozen or more are very rare, or quite unknown, in the south. I once lived for several years on the hills above Chesterfield, a good way to the east of this limestone country; and to visit the nearest of the Dales there was a walk of seven miles, to and fro, across the intervening high moors that form the southern buttress of the Pennines. Stoney Middleton is far from being one of the pleasantest of Peakland villages; but such was the interest of its flora that the fourteen-mile trudge, and more, was often undertaken during the summer months.

After traversing the great heathery moors devoted to the cult of the grouse, and descending from the rocky rampart of gritstone known as Curbar Edge, one crosses the valley of the Derwent; and here a pause may be made to notice a patch of sweet Cicely, one of the loveliest of the umbelliferous tribe. It is a charming sight, as it stands up tall in the sunshine, with its soft feathery cream-white masses of foliage and its fernlike leaflets; too fair and fragile, it would seem, for human hands, for it droops very soon if cut. Every part of it—stalk, leaves, flowers, and fruit—has the same aromatic fragrance (its local name is "anise"), and so gracious is it to sight, scent, and touch, that one longs to bathe one's senses in its luxuriance.

Middleton Dale, naturally beautiful, but sadly deformed by lime-kilns, is famous for a cliff known as the Lover's Leap, from which an enamoured maiden is said to have thrown herself down. Had it been the love of flowers, rather than of man, that tempted her to that dizzy verge, there would have been no cause for surprise; for there are many alluring plants on the ledges of the scarp, including a brilliant show of wild wallflowers. In May and June there may be found along the northern side of the dale the yellow petals of the spring cinquefoil (*potentilla verna*), a gem of a flower, which, in Mr. Reginald Farrer's words, "clings to the white cliff-face, and from far off you see a splash of gold on the greyness." A month later the equally attractive Nottingham catch-fly (*silene nutans*) will be abundant on the rocks; a plant of nocturnal habits which expands its petals and becomes fragrant in the evening, but "nods," as its Latin name avows, in the daytime, when it wears a sleepy and somewhat dissipated look, like a wassailer—a white campion that has been "on spree." By night its beauty is beyond cavil.

On the lower slopes is a colony of a still stranger-looking flower, the woolly-headed thistle, whose involucre is so bulky, and its scales so densely wrapped in white down, that it has an almost grotesque appearance, as of a thistle with "swelled head." It is, however, a very handsome plant; and when growing in vast numbers, as I have seen it in one of its special haunts, near Wychwood Forest, in Oxfordshire, it makes a glorious spectacle.

Of the three species of saxifrages—the rue-leaved, the meadow, and the mossy—that thrive along the bottom of the dale, the two former are southern as well as northern flowers; but the presence of the mossy saxifrage is a sign that we are in a mountainous region, and as such it is always welcome. With these grows the graceful vernal sandwort, another flower of the hills, and so often the companion of saxifrages that it is naturally associated with them in the mind.

But Middleton Dale, the nearest to my starting-point, and therefore the most frequently visited by me, is much surpassed in floral wealth by the long valley of the Wye, which in its course from Buxton to Bakewell bears the names successively of Wye Dale, Chee Dale, Miller's Dale, and Monsal Dale. In one or another of these four glens nearly all the rarer limestone flowers have their station. You may find, for instance, three very local crucifers: the two whitlow-grasses, *draba incana* and *draba muralis*, remarkable only as being scarce in other parts of the kingdom; and the really beautiful little *Hutchinsia*, with its tiny white blossoms and finely cut pinnate leaves. Jacob's-ladder, a handsome blue flower, very uncommon in a wild state, is also native on the bluffs and slopes in Chee Dale and elsewhere: in fact a stroll along almost any of the limestone escarpments will bring new treasures to sight.

But the flower which I best love is one which grows by the streamside—in Wye Dale it is in profusion—the modest water-avens, often strangely undervalued by writers who describe it as "dingy." Thus in Delamer's *The Flower Garden* it is stated that this avens "is more remarkable for having been one of the favourites, the whims, the caprices of the great Linnæus, than for anything else: it is hard to say what, in a British meadow-weed, could so take the fancy of the Master." Was ever such blindness of eye, such hardness of heart? And the wiseacre goes on to say that "it is impossible to account, logically, for attachments and sympathies."

Logic, truly, would be out of place in such a connection; but it is not difficult to understand Linnæus's feelings towards the water-avens. There is a rare beauty in the droop of its bell-like head, and in its soft and subdued tints—the deep rufous brown of the long sepals, through which peep the silky petals in hues that range from creamy white to vinous red, and all steeped in a quiet radiance as of some old stained glass. I must own to thinking it the most tenderly beautiful of all English wildflowers. The hybrid between the water-avens and the common avens is occasionally found by the Wye: one which I saw in Miller's Dale had green sepals and petals of pale yellow.

The Alpine penny-cress (*thlaspi alpestre*), a crucifer native on limestone rocks, may be seen on the High Tor at Matlock, where it grows with the vernal sandwort on débris at the mouth of caves; a graceful little plant with white flowers and a smooth unbranched stem so closely clasped by the narrow leaves as to give it the look of a perfoliate.

One other limestone district shall be mentioned; the hills round Castleton. Cave Dale, approached by a narrow gorge close to the village, is well worth the flower-lover's attention; for bleak and bare as it is, its slippery sides harbour some interesting plants, such as the mountain rue (*thalictrum minus*), and the scurvy-grass (*cochlearia alpina*), both in considerable quantity. In the Winnatts, too, the steep ravine which overhangs the road from Castleton to Chapel-en-le-Frith, one may find Jacob's-ladder and other rarities on the rocks; and the gorgeous mountain pansy (*viola lutea*) is not far distant on the upland heaths and pastures.

The list is far from being exhausted; but enough has been said to show that there is no lack of entertainment among these limestone dales. To enter one of them, after crossing the moorland from the dreary coal district of east Derbyshire, is like stepping from penury to plenty, from wilderness to paradise: there is a change of colouring that instantly attracts the eye. Even in early spring the little shining crane's-bill decks the walls and lower rocks with its rose-petaled flowers; and at midsummer the more showy stonecrop flings a veritable cloth of gold over the crags and lawns. Few localities present so many charming flowers in so limited a space.

And now let us turn from the limestone valleys to those of the millstone grit.

The controversy as to which part of Derbyshire best deserves the name of "The Peak" has always seemed a vain one, not merely because there is no peak in the county at all, but because no connoisseur can doubt for a moment that the district which alone has the true characteristics of a mountain is the great triangular plateau of gritstone known as Kinderscout. Less beautiful than the limestone dales, with their beetling crags and wealth of flowers, the wilder region surrounding "the Scout" has the advantage of being a real bit of mountain scenery, topped as it is with black "tors" and "towers" that rise out of the heather, and flanked with rocky "edges" from which its steep "cloughs" descend into the valleys below.

Unfortunately, this great rocky tableland has of late years become almost a *terra incognita* to the nature-lover, as a result of the agreement which was made, after prolonged controversy, between the Peak District Society and the grouse-shooting landlords, inasmuch as, while permitting the traveller to skirt the shoulders of the hill, it excluded him wholly from its summit.

With the exception of the heather, the bilberry, and a few kindred species, the plants of the gritstone hills are sparse; but there is one, the cloudberry—so-called, according to Gerarde's rather magniloquent description, because "it groweth naturally upon the tops of high mountains ... where the clouds are lower than the tops of the same all winter long"—which well repays a pilgrimage. It is a prostrate and spineless bramble (*rubus chamæmorus*), highly valued in northern countries for its rich orange-coloured fruit. It grows thickly on the ground, making a dark-green patch in marked contrast to the coarse herbage; and towards the end of June one may see a profusion of the large white blossoms and a few early formed berries at the same time. There is a good-sized plot of it near the summit of the pass that crosses the shoulder of Kinder Scout from Edale Head.

But of the plants that grow on the Scout itself I am unable to speak; for my only visit to it—not reckoning an unsuccessful attempt when I was turned back by a keeper—took place in the depth of a very snowy winter. It was on the afternoon of a frosty January day, when the sun was already low, that in the company of my friend Bertram Lloyd, and armed with a passport, in the form of a letter of permission, given us by the courtesy of one of the owners of the shooting, I climbed from Edale, through the region of right-of-way into that of flagrant trespass. We felt an unusual sense of legality, as we passed a weather-beaten notice-board, with a half-obliterated threat that trespassers would be "—cuted," whether executed, electrocuted, or prosecuted was left to the imagination of the offender; and I think the strangeness of his position was rather embarrassing to my companion, who is such a confirmed trespasser that he feels as if something must be amiss unless there is a gamekeeper to be reckoned with—like the mountain ram, in Thompson-Seton's story, who was so accustomed to be hunted that he became moody and restless when his pursuer was not in sight.

But, at the time of our visit, no passport was demanded; for the keepers, like the grouse themselves, appeared to have deserted the heights for the valleys. Indeed, hardly any life at all was to be seen, with the exception of a grey mountain hare, couched upon a stack of rock, who regarded us with a mild and curious eye as we passed some two hundred feet above him, and seemed to be satisfied that we were harmless. Nor was this lack of life surprising, for a more desolate scene could hardly be imagined—a great snow-clad "moss," intersected by deep ruts, which, being choked with snow, had somewhat of the appearance of crevasses, and punctuated here and there with the black masonry of the tors. From the highest point that we reached, marked in the ordnance map as 2,088 feet, there was a wonderful sunset view, though the Manchester district that lies to the west of the Scout was hidden in lurid fog. It is said that Snowdon, a hundred miles distant, has been seen from this point. It was certainly not visible upon the occasion to which I refer.

It is impossible to visit this high mountain plateau, lying as it does at about an equal distance from Manchester and Sheffield, without feeling that what is now a private grouse-moor must, before many years have passed, become a nationalized park or "reservation"—a playground for the dwellers in the great Midland cities, and a sanctuary for wild animals and plants.

The time will assuredly come when the sport of the few will have to give way to the health and recreation of the many.

## XV
## NO THOROUGHFARE!

Trespassers will be prosecuted.

THE subject of trespassing mentioned in the preceding chapter, has a very close and personal interest for the adventurous flower-lover; for of all incentives to ignore the familiar notice-board with its hackneyed words of warning, none perhaps is more potent than the possibility that some rare and long-sought wildflower is to be found on the forbidden land. The appeal is one that no explorer can resist. If "stout Cortez" himself, when with eagle eyes he stared at the Pacific, had seen that ocean labelled as "strictly private and preserved," could he have desisted from his quest?

There is moreover a good deal to be said in extenuation of trespassing as a summer recreation; and if landlords go on at their present rate, in closing footpaths and excluding the public from green fields and hedgerows, trespassing will perhaps establish itself as one of our recognized national diversions. Hitherto, it must be confessed, it has remained to some extent in disrepute; doubtless, through its being so largely indulged in by poachers and other evil-doers, who have given a bad name to a practice which in itself is innocent and blameless enough. Most people, especially landlords and gamekeepers, have a fixed belief that a trespasser's purpose must be a lawless and mischievous one. Why so? Is it not possible that some trespassers may have other objects than to steal pheasants' eggs or snare rabbits? If huntsmen when following the hounds are permitted, not only to trespass, but to damage crops and fences, why should the naturalist be molested when harmlessly following his own inclinations in choice of a country ramble. Is the pursuit of the fox a surer proof of honest intentions than the pursuit of natural history? It appears that some landowners think so. "Trespassers will be prosecuted," say the notices that everywhere stare us in the face.

Was there ever such a lying legend? Trespassers will *not* be prosecuted, for the sufficient reason that in English law trespassing is not an offence. Of course, if any injury be done to property, the owner can sue for damages, but a harmless trespasser can only be requested to depart, though, if he be ill-advised enough to refuse to go, he may be forcibly ejected. We see, therefore, that the threatened "prosecution" of trespassers is in reality merely a *brutum fulmen* launched by landlords at a too credulous public, a pious fraud which has been far more efficacious than such kindred notices as "Beware the dog," or "Beware the bull," though these, too, have done good service in their time. Trespassers will not be prosecuted, provided that they do no sort of damage, and that if their presence is objected to they politely retire. With these slight precautions and limitations, a trespasser may go where he will, and enjoy the study of Nature in her most secluded and "strictly private" recesses. He thus himself becomes, in one sense, a lord of the soil; but his domain is far more extensive and unencumbered than that of any actual landlord. He enjoys all that is best in park, woodland, or mountain; and if he is "warned off" one estate he can afford to smile at the prohibition, since many other regions are open to him, and he can confidently look forward to a visit to fresh woods and pastures new on the morrow.

In the course of these rambles the trespasser will probably, like Ulysses, have some curious experiences of men and of notice-boards. It is very instructive to observe the various types of the landlord class, and their different methods of treating the intruder whom they meet on their fields. There is the indignant landlord, who can scarcely conceal his wrath at the astounding audacity of one who is deliberately crossing his land without having come "on business." There is the despairing landlord, who has been so broken by previous invasions that he is now content with a shrug of the shoulders and a remark that the place is "quite private, you know." There is the courteous landlord, who politely assumes that you have lost your way, and naively offers to conduct you to the high-road by the shortest cut; and there is the mildly ironical, who, as in a case which I remember on a Surrey hillside, remarks as he passes you: "There goes my heather."

I have heard it said that one can sometimes divine the character of a landlord from the wording of his notice-boards, and I believe from my own experiences that there is truth in the idea. Certainly the notice-board is the landlord's favourite method of defending the privacy of his estate, and for obvious reasons; for not only is it the least troublesome and expensive way of conveying the desired warning to would-be trespassers, but the salutary fiction regarding the "prosecution" of offenders is thus publicly and permanently impressed on the agricultural mind. There is not such entire uniformity in the wording of notice-boards as might be supposed. Of course by far the commonest form is the well-known "No thoroughfare. Trespassers will be prosecuted as the law directs," in which the unconscious irony contained in the last four words has always struck me as especially delightful. To this is often added the words "and all dogs shot," in which the experienced trespasser will detect signs of a certain roughness and inhumanity of temperament on the part of the owner. More original forms of expression are by no means uncommon. Sometimes the warning is emphasized by the bold statement, indicating the possession by the landlord of humorous or imaginative faculties, that "the police have orders to watch." Sometimes, but more rarely, the personal element is boldly introduced, as in the assertion, which might formerly be seen on a notice-board in one of the most beautiful valleys of the Lake District, "This is my land. Trespassers, etc." In some cases the wording has evidently been left to the care of subordinates, and hence result some curiosities of literary composition. "Private. Beware of dogs," is an instance of this kind, in which the ambiguity of the allusion to dogs, whether those of the landlord or the trespasser, seems almost oracular. In these and other ways a certain zest is lent to the excursions or rather the *in*cursions, of the trespasser, which lifts them above the level of ordinary walking exercise.

In the case of wealthy landowners, the duty of warning off the trespasser devolves on gamekeepers, who, being less emotional than their employers, are a far less interesting study. Stolid and furry, and apparently endowed with only the animal instincts of the victims whom they delight in tracking and trapping, they are by far the least intelligent people whom the trespasser encounters; they are, in fact, no better than breathing and walking notice-boards, with the disadvantage that they cannot be so absolutely disregarded. It is unwise to argue with them; for reason is at a discount in such encounters and there is the possibility, in some districts, of their having recourse to personal violence, in the knowledge that if the matter should come before local magistrates the keeper's word would be honoured in preference to that of the trespasser. There is a sanctity in the word "Preserve."

An experience of this sort actually befell a friend of mine, who himself narrated it in print. A devoted botanist and nature-lover, he was twice in the same day found trespassing by a gigantic gamekeeper, who, on the second occasion, ended all parley in the manner described in the following "Mystical Ballad," wherein the writer has ventured somewhat to idealize the circumstances, though the story is based on the facts.

I have often thought it was an error on the part of the trespassing poet not to explain to his assailant that he was a botanist; for "botanist," as I can testify, is a blessed word which has a soothing effect upon many of the most irascible landowners or their satellites. Personally I never presume to call myself botanist, except when I am found trespassing, on which occasions I have rarely known it to fail. I recall a Saturday afternoon when, as I was rambling in a Derbyshire dale with Bertram Lloyd, and admiring the flowers, we were accosted by the owner in person, who inquired with a sort of suppressed fury whether we knew that we were on his estate. We said we were botanists, and the effect was magical; in less than a minute we were courteously permitted to go where we would and stay as long as we liked.

For botany is regarded as a scientific study; and even sportsmen do not like to incur the reproach of being enemies to science. Their better feelings may be conveyed in a familiar Virgilian line: *Non obtusa adeo gestamus pectora Pœni.*

# XVI
## LIMESTONE COASTS AND CLIFFS

A LIMESTONE soil is everywhere rich in flowers—we have seen what the midland dales can produce—but it is especially so in the close neighbourhood of the sea. Two instances suggest themselves; one from a Carnarvonshire promontory, the Orme's Head; the other from Arnside Knott, in Westmorland.

Fifty years ago the Great Orme was a wild and picturesque headland, girdled by a footpath which made a circuit of the beetling cliffs, and crossed by a few other tracks leading to the telegraph station at the summit, St. Tudno's Church, and elsewhere; but in most respects still in a primitive and unimpaired condition. I knew almost every yard of it as a boy; and I remember, among other attractions, a hermit who lived in a cave, and better still a wild cat— probably a fugitive from some Llandudno lodging-house— who had her home in a stack of rocks on the western side of the Head. On the western shore of the isthmus there was at that time only one house; it belonged to Dean Liddell, famous as joint author of the Greek dictionary distressfully known to generations of students as *Liddell and Scott.*

But now, owing to the "development" of Llandudno, this once beautiful foreland has become a place almost of horror, vulgarized by trams, motor-roads, golf-links, and all the appurtenances of "civilization;" and were it not for the wildflowers, it might well be shunned by those who knew it in old days. Flowers, however, are very tenacious of their established haunts, and the remark made in Mr. J. E. Griffith's *Flora of Carnarvonshire* still holds good, that "the flora of this district is quite unique, in consequence of the number of species found here, and the rarity of many of them." The luxuriance of the flowers is indeed a sight which can almost make one forget the "improvements" that have ruined the scenery.

Among the plants inhabiting the rocky banks above the shore are the blue vernal squill, the sea stork's-bill, sweet alyssum, hound's-tongue, hemlock, henbane, mullein, and tree-mallow: to these may be added what constitutes a herb-garden readymade—fennel, wormwood, vervain, white horehound, wild sage, succory, and Alexanders. On the higher cliffs are the curious samphire, pink thrift, white scurvy-grass, and great tufts of sea-cabbage, now rarer and more local than formerly, but here waving its pale yellow pennons in abundance. Most charming of all, the brilliant blood-red crane's-bill, together with two kinds of rock-rose (the hoary dwarf species as well as the common one), makes rich splashes of colour on the grey limestone ledges. A little back from the sea, among the bluffs that overhang the town, you may light upon the sleepy-looking catch-fly (*silene nutans*); the tiny Hutchinsia; and in one or two places the shrub cotoneaster, which is said to be native only upon the Great Orme. I have, however, seen it growing apparently wild at Capel Curig, and at a greater distance from houses than in its Llandudno station.

Nor is it only the Great Orme that shows this floral wealth: the Little Orme has the rare Welsh stonecrop (*sedum Forsterianum*); and on another height in the same district, the small circular hill known as Deganwy Rocks, there is a profusion of flowers. When I revisited it a few years ago, not having set foot on it for nearly half a century, I found that the villas of Deganwy had crept up almost to the base of the rocks, and on another side there was—still worse—a camp of German prisoners, with armed sentries supervising their labours; yet even there, close above such scenes, were growing plants which might mark a memorable day in the annals of a flower-lover, notably the maiden pink and the milk-thistle—the "holy" thistle, as it is not inaptly called. The pinks, a lovely band, were sprinkled along the turf at the foot of the rocks; the thistles were almost at the top; between them on a stony ledge nestled a quantity of viper's bugloss, and with it some borage, two kindred plants which I had never before seen in company.

Nearly all the members of the Borage group are interesting—lungwort, alkanet, forget-me-not, hound's-tongue, and bugloss—but the borage itself, a roadside weed in South Europe, and in this country merely an immigrant and "casual," is to me the most precious of all. My earliest recollections of it, I must own, are as an ingredient of claret-cup at Cambridge, its silver-grey stems floating in the wine with a pleasant roughness to the lip; but in those unregenerate days we did not know the real virtue of the herb, famous from old time, as Gerarde says, for its power "to exhilarate and make the mind glad, to comfort the heart, and for driving away of sorrow." And certainly, in another and better use, it *does* comfort the heart and drive sorrow away; for its "gallant blew flowers" are of all blues the loveliest, and the black anthers give it a peculiarly poignant look which reminds one somehow of the wistfulness of a Gainsborough portrait. In the list of my best-beloved flowers it ranks among the highest.

Looking north-east from the Orme's Head, one may see on a clear day, across some sixty miles of water, the limestone hills of Westmorland, reckoned as part of Lakeland, but geologically, botanically, and in general character a quite separate district. Arnside Knott, a bluff overlooking the estuary of the river Kent where it widens into Morecambe Bay, is the presiding genius of a tract of shore and forest to which the name of "Lily-land" has been given by Mr. J. A. Barnes in a sketch of Arnside, and which he describes as "a perfect paradise of wildflowers." Let us suppose ourselves transported thither, and see how the claim holds good.

The lily of the valley is one of those favoured plants which are everywhere highly esteemed; even the man who in general cares but little for wildflowers takes this one to his heart, or, what is worse, to his garden. I have already quoted Mr. C. A. Johns's queer appreciation of this native British wildflower as "a universally admired garden plant." On the wooded hill known as Arnside Park the "May lily," as it used to be called (and here it is certainly not "of the valley"), covers many acres of ground, and justifies the title "Lily-land" as applied to the Arnside neighbourhood. What I found still more interesting was an almost equal abundance of the stone bramble (*rubus saxatilis*), which grows intermixed with the lilies over a large portion of the wood.

On these Westmorland Cliffs, as in those of Carnarvonshire, the blood-red crane's-bill is conspicuous, but it is much less plentiful, nor are the outstanding flowers of the two localities the same. One of the commonest at Arnside is the tall ploughman's spikenard, known locally as "frankincense": and on the lawns that skirt the Knott one often sees the mountain-cudweed or "cat's-foot," the gromwell or "grey millet," and the beautiful little dwarf orchis. The district is rather rich in orchids; among others, I found the rare narrow-leaved helleborine (*cephalanthera ensifolia*) in the Arnside woods. The deadly nightshade is frequent; so, too, is the four-leaved herb-Paris, which a resident described to me as being here "almost a weed." But there are two other flowers that demand more special mention.

In a lane near Arnside Tower, a ruin that lies below the Knott on its inland side, there is a considerable growth of green hellebore, apparently at the very spot where its presence was recorded two centuries ago. Though not a very rare plant, it is extremely local; and owing to its strongly marked features, the large palmate leaves and pale green flowers, is not likely to go unnoticed.

But the rarest of Arnside flowers is, or was, another poisonous plant of the *ranunculus* order, the baneberry, for which the writer of "Lily-land," as he tells us, "hunted for years without success; till its exact locality was at last revealed to me by one who knew, in a situation so obvious that I felt like a man who has hunted through every room in the house for the spectacles on his own nose." Years later, on my certifying that I was not a knight of the trowel, Mr. Barnes was so kind as to confide to me this same secret that had been kept hidden from the uninitiate; but I found that the small plantation which had been the home of the baneberry, almost within Arnside itself, had recently been cut down, and though a few of the plants were still growing along the side of the field, they had ceased to flower, and possibly by this time they have ceased to exist. Even as it was, I felt myself fortunate to have seen the baneberry in one of its few native haunts. The pale green deeply cut leaves are much handsomer than those of its relatives the hellebore and the monk's-hood. Its raceme of white flowers and its black berries are also known to me; but alas, only in a garden.

Where flowers are concerned, there is little truth in the saying that "comparisons are odious"; on the contrary it is both pleasant and profitable to compare not only plant with plant, but the flora of one fertile district with that of another. The natural scenery of Arnside is yet unspoilt, and for that reason it now offers greater attractions to the nature-lover than the ruined charms of Llandudno; but if he were asked, for botanical reasons only, to choose between a visit to the Orme and a visit to the Knott, the decision might be a less easy one. "How happy could I be with either!" would probably be his thought.

# XVII
## ON PILGRIMAGE TO INGLEBOROUGH

THERE is a tale by Herman Melville which deals with the strangeness of a first meeting between the inmates of two houses which face each other, far and high away, on opposite mountain ranges, and yet, though daily visible, have remained for years as mutually unknown as if they belonged to different worlds. It was with this story in my mind that I approached for the first time the moorland mass of Ingleborough, long familiar as seen from the Lake mountains, a square-topped height on the horizon to the south-east, but hitherto unvisited by me owing to the more imperious claims of the Great Gable and Scafell. But now, at last, I found myself on pilgrimage to Ingleborough; the impulse, long delayed, had seized me to stand on the summit of the Yorkshire fell, and, looking north-westward, to see the scene reversed.

Another of Ingleborough's attractions was that it is the home of certain scarce and beautiful flowers, as has been pointed out in Mr. Reginald Farrer's interesting books on Alpine plants. Such exceptional rarities as the baneberry (*actæa spicata*), which grows among rocky crevices high up on the fell—not to mention the *arenaria gothica*, choicest of the sandworts—the mere visitor can hardly hope to discover; but there are other and less infrequent treasures upon the hill, beyond which my ambition did not aspire.

As I ascended the barren marshy slopes that form the eastern flank, I realized once again how much more the labour of an ascent depends upon the character of the ground than upon the actual height to be scaled. Ingleborough is under 2,400 feet; yet it is far more toilsome to climb than many a rocky peak in Wales or Cumberland that rises hundreds of feet higher, and it is a relief at length to get a firm foothold on the rocks of millstone grit which form the summit. Thence, from the edges which drop sharply from the flat top, one looks out on the somewhat desolate fells stretching away on three sides—Pen-y-ghent to the east, Whernside to the north, and to the south the more distant forest of Pendle—but westward there is the gleam of sand or water in Morecambe Bay, and the eye hastens to greet the dim but ever glorious forms of the Lakeland mountains.

In the affections of the mountain-lover Ingleborough can never be the rival of one of these; indeed, in the strict sense, it is not a mountain at all, but a high moor built on a base of limestone with a cap of grit. Still, there is grandeur in the steep scarps that guard its central stronghold; and its dark summit, when viewed from a distance crowning the successive tiers of grey terraces, has a strength and wildness of its own, and even suggests at points a likeness to the massive tower of the Great Gable. To one looking down from the topmost edges on the scattered piles of limestone below, the effect is very curious. You see, perhaps, a mile or two distant, what looks at first sight like a flock of sheep at pasture, but is soon discovered to be a stone flock which has no mortal shepherd. In other parts are wide white plateaux which, when visited, turn out to be a wilderness of low flat rocks, everywhere weather-worn and water-worn, scooped and scalloped into cells and basins, and so intersected by channels filled with ferns and grasses that one has to walk warily over it as over a reef at low tide.

But to return to the flowers. At the summit were mossy saxifrage and vernal sandwort; and on the cliffs just below, to the western side, the big mountain stonecrop, rose-root, not unhandsome with its yellow blossoms, flourished in some abundance, even as it did when Gerarde wrote of it, nearly three hundred years ago. The purple saxifrage, an early spring flower, is also found on these rocks, but at the time when I visited the spot, in late June, its blossoming season was over, and nothing was visible but the leaves. There was little else but some hawkweeds; I turned my attention, therefore, to the flowers of the lower slopes.

There is nothing more delightful, in descending a mountain, than to follow the leading of some rapid beck from its very source to the valley; and it is rather disconcerting, in these limestone regions, that the cavernous nature of the ground should make the presence of the streams so intermittent, and that one's chosen companion should not unfrequently disappear, just when his value is most appreciated, into some "gaping gill" or pot-hole.

It is said of Walt Whitman that sometimes when a pilgrim was privileged to walk with him, and was perhaps thinking that their acquaintance was ripening to friendship, the good grey poet, with a curt nod and a careless "good-bye," would turn off abruptly and be gone. Even so it is with these wayward streams that course down the sides of Ingleborough. Just when one is on the best of terms with them, they vanish and are no more.

But with the bird's-eye primrose tinging hillsides and hollows with its tender hue of pink, no other companionship was needed. A mountain flower, it is the fairest of all the

*Primulaceæ*, that band of fair sisters to which it belongs—primrose, cowslip, pimpernel, loosestrife, and money-wort—all beautiful and all favourites among young and old alike, whereever there is a love of flowers. It was worthwhile to make the pilgrimage to Ingleborough, if only to see this charming little plant in perfection on its native banks.

Nor were other flowers lacking; the wild geraniums especially were in force. The shining crane's-bill gleamed on the pale limestone ledges; the wood crane's-bill, a local North-country species, gave a glint of purple in the copses at the foot of the fell; and still further down, below the village of Clapham, there were masses of the blue meadow crane's-bill (*geranium pratense*), the largest and not least handsome of the family. The water-avens was everywhere by the stream sides; and on a bank above the road the gladdon, or purple iris, was opening its dull-tinted flowers.

# XVIII
## A BOTANOPHILIST'S JOURNAL

I HAVE referred several times to Henry Thoreau, of Concord, in whose *Journal* a great deal is said about wildflowers; and as the volumes are not easily accessible to English readers it may be worthwhile to select therefrom a few of the more interesting passages. In all that he wrote on the subject Thoreau appears less as the botanist than the flower-lover; indeed, he expressly observes that he himself comes under the head of the "Botanophilists," as Linnæus termed them; viz. those who record various facts about flowers, but not from a strictly scientific standpoint. "I never studied botany," he said, "and do not to-day, systematically; the most natural system is so artificial. I wanted to know my neighbours, if possible; to get a little nearer to them." So great was his zest in cultivating this floral acquaintance that, as he tells us, he often visited a plant four or five miles from Concord half a dozen times within a fortnight, in order to note its time of flowering.

Books he found, in general, unsatisfactory. "I asked a learned and accurate naturalist," he says, "who is at the same time the courteous guardian of a public library, to direct me to those works which contained the more particular popular account, or *biography*, of particular flowers—for I had trusted that each flower had had many lovers and faithful describers in past times—but he informed me that I had read all; that no one was acquainted with them, they were only catalogued

98

like his books." It was the human aspect of the flower that Thoreau craved; and he was therefore disappointed when he saw "pages about some fair flower's qualities as food or medicine, but perhaps not a sentence about its significance to the eye; as if the cowslip were better for 'greens' than for yellows." Thus he complained that botanies are "the prose of flowers," instead of what they ought to be, the poetry. He made an exception, however, in favour of old Gerarde's *Herball*.

His admirable though quaint descriptions are, to my mind, greatly superior to the modern more scientific ones. He describes not according to rule, but to his natural delight in the plants. He brings them vividly before you, as one who has seen and delighted in them. It is almost as good as to see the plants themselves. His leaves are leaves; his flowers, flowers; his fruit, fruit. They are green, and coloured, and fragrant. It is a man's knowledge added to a child's delight. . . . How much better to describe your object in fresh English words rather than in these conventional Latinisms!"

Linnæus, too, "the man of flowers," as he calls him, is praised by Thoreau. "If you would read books on botany, go to the fathers of the science. Read Linnæus at once, and come down from him as far as you please. I lost much time in reading the florists. It is remarkable how little the mass of those interested in botany are acquainted with Linnæus."

Thoreau's manner of botanizing was, like most of his habits, somewhat singular. His vasculum was his straw-hat. "I never used any other," he writes, "and when some whom I visited were evidently surprised at its dilapidated look, as I deposited it on their front entry-table, I assured them it was not so much my hat as my botany-box." With this vasculum he professed himself more than content.

I am inclined to think that my hat, whose lining is gathered in midway so as to make a shelf, is about as good a botany-box as I could have; and there is something in the darkness and the vapours that arise from the head—at least, if you take a bath—which preserves flowers through a long walk. Flowers will frequently come fresh out of this botany-box at the end of the day, though they have had no sprinkling.

The joy of meeting with a new plant, a sensation known to all searchers after flowers, is more than once mentioned in the *Journal*: the discovery of a single flower hitherto unknown to him makes him feel as if he were in a wealth of novelties. "By the discovery of one new plant all bounds seem to be infinitely removed." He notes, too, the not uncommon experience, that a flower, once recognized, is likely soon to be re-encountered. Seeing something blue, or glaucous, in a swamp, he approaches it, and finds it to be the *Andromeda polifolia*, which had been shown him, only a few days before, in Emerson's collection; now he sees it in abundance. At times he adopts the method of sitting quietly and looking around him, on the principle that "as it is best to sit in a grove and let the birds come to you, so, as it were, even the flowers will come."

Swamps were among Thoreau's favourite haunts: he thinks it would be a luxury to stand in one, up to his chin, for a whole summer's day, scenting the sweet-fern and bilberries. "That is a glorious swamp of Miles's," he remarks; "the more open parts, where the dwarf andromeda prevails. . . . These are the wildest and richest gardens that we have." The fields were less trustworthy, because of the annual vandalism of the mowing. "About these times," he writes in June, "some hundreds of men, with freshly sharpened scythes, make an irruption into my garden when in its rankest condition, and clip my herbs all as close as they can; and I am restricted to the rough hedges and worn-out fields which had little to attract them."

Among Thoreau's best-beloved flowers, if we may judge by certain passages of the *Journal*, was the large white bindweed (*convolvulus sepium*), or morning-glory." "It always refreshes me to see it," he writes; "I associate it with holiest morning hours. It may preside over my morning walks and thoughts." Not less worthily celebrated by him, in another mood, are the wild rose and the water-lily.

We now have roses on the land and lilies on the water— both land and water have done their best—now, just after the longest day. Nature says, "You behold the utmost I can do." The red rose, with the intense colour of many suns concentrated, spreads its tender petals perfectly fair, its flower not to be overlooked, modest yet queenly, on the edges of shady copses and meadows.... And the water-lily floats on the smooth surface of slow waters, amid rounded shields of leaves, bucklers, red beneath, which simulate a green field, perfuming the air. The highest, intensest colour belongs to the land; the purest, perchance, to the water.

It was not Thoreau's practice to pluck many flowers; he preferred, as a rule, to leave them where they were; but he speaks of the fitness of having "in a vase of water on your table the wildflowers of the season which are just blossoming": thus in mid-June he brings home some rosebuds ready to expand, "and the next morning they open and fill my chamber with fragrance." At another time the grateful thought of the calamint's scent suffices him: "I need not smell it; it is a balm to my mind to remember its fragrance."

It was characteristic of Thoreau that he loved to renew his outdoor pleasures in remembrance, by pondering over the beautiful things he had witnessed, whether through sight or sound or scent. His mountain excursions were not fully apprehended by him, until he had afterwards meditated on them. "It is after we get home," he says, "that we really go over the mountain, if ever. What did the mountain say? What did the mountain do?" So it was with his flowers: even in the long winter evenings they were still his companions and friends.

On a January date we find him writing in his *Journal*: "Perhaps what most moves us in winter is some reminiscence of far-off summer. How we leap by the side of the open brooks! What life, what society! The cold is merely superficial; it is summer still at the core."

# XIX
## FELONS AND OUTLAWS

THAT there are felonious as well as philanthropic flowers, plants that are actively malignant in their relation to mankind, has always been a popular belief. The upas-tree, for example, has given rise to many gruesome stories; and the mandrake, fabled to shriek when torn from the ground, has played a frequent part in poetry and legend; not to mention the host of noxious weeds, the "plants at whose names the verse feels loath," as Shelley has it:

And thistles, and nettles, and darnels rank,

And the dock, and henbane, and hemlock dank.

The felons, however, of whom I would now speak are not the plants that seem merely foul and repulsive, such as the docks and nettles, the broom-rapes, toothworts, and similar ill-looking parasites, but rather the bold bad outlaws and highwaymen, the "gentlemen of the road," who, however deleterious to human welfare, have a sinister beauty and distinction of their own, and are thus able to fascinate us. Prominent among these is the clan of the nightshades, to which the mandrake itself belongs, and which has several well-known representatives among British flowers; above all, the deadly nightshade, or dwale, as it is better named, to distinguish it from smaller relatives that are wrongly described as "the deadly." So poisonous is the dwale that Gerarde three centuries ago exhorted his readers to "banish these pernicious plants out of your gardens, and all places near to your houses, where children do resort;" and modern writers tell us that the plant is "fortunately" of rare occurrence. But threatened plants, like threatened men, live long; and the dwale, though very local, may still be found in some abundance: there are woods where it grows even in profusion, and, *pace* Gerarde, rejoices the heart of the flower-lover, for in truth it has a strange and ominous charm, this massive grave-looking plant with the large oval leaves, heavy sombre purple blossoms, and big black "wolf-cherries."

Next to the dwale in the nightshade family must rank the henbane, a fallen angel among wildflowers; for its beauty is of the sickly and fetid kind, which at once attracts and repels. It is curious that in the lines from Shelley's "Sensitive Plant" the epithet "dank" should be given to the hemlock, to which it is quite unsuited, rather than to the henbane, where its appropriateness could not be questioned; for the stalk, leaves, and flowers of the henbane are alike clammy to the touch. Presumably this uncertain and sporadic herb has become rarer of late years; for whereas it is frequently stated in books to be "common in waste places," one may visit hundreds of waste places without a glimpse of it. In the *Flora of the Lake District* (1885) Arnside is given as one of its localities; but I was told by a resident that he had only once seen it there, and then it had sprung up in his garden.

It is in similar places that the thorn-apple, another cousin to the nightshade, is apt to make its un-invited appearance; less a felon, perhaps, than a sturdy rogue and vagabond among flowers of ill repute. A year or two ago, I was told by the holder of an allotment-garden that a great number of thorn-apples were springing up in his ground; and knowing my interest in flowers he sent me a small basketful of the young plants, which, rather to my neighbours' surprise, I set

104

out in a row, like lettuces, in a corner of my back-yard. There they flourished well, and in due course made a fine show with their trumpet-shaped white flowers and the big thorny capsules whence the plant takes its name. It is not a bad-looking fellow, but awkward and hulking, and quite devoid of the sickly grace of the henbane or of the bodeful gloom of the dwale.

Passing now to the handsome but acrid tribe of the *ranunculi*, and omitting the poisonous but interesting baneberry, of which I have already spoken, we come to two formidable plants, the hellebore and the monk's-hood, which have been famous from earliest times for their dangerous propensities. The green hellebore, though in Westmorland named "felon grass," is a less felonious-looking flower than its close kinsman the fetid hellebore, whose general appearance, owing to the crude pale green of its purple-tipped sepals, and the reluctance of its globe-like buds to expand themselves fully, is one of insalubrity and unripeness. But it is a plant of distinction, some two or three feet in height; and as it flowers before the winter is well past, it can hardly fail to arrest attention in the few places where it is to be found: in Arundel Park, in Sussex, it may be seen growing in close conjunction with the deadly nightshade—a noteworthy pair of desperadoes.

The other malefactor of the ranunculus family is the aconite, or monk's-hood, a poisonous but very picturesque flower with deep blue blossoms, which takes its name from the hood-like appearance of the upper sepal. "It beareth," Gerarde tells us, "very fair and goodly blew floures in shape like a helmet, which are so beautiful that a man would thinke they were of some excellent vertue." A traitor, a masked bandit it is, of such evil reputation that, according to Pliny, it kills man, "unless it can find in him something else to kill," some disease, to wit; and thus it holds its place in the pharmacopœia.

The umbellifers include a number of outlaws such as the water-dropworts and cowbane; but among the dangerous members of the tribe there is only one that attains to real greatness, and that of course is the hemlock, a poisoner of old-established renown, as witness the death of Socrates. "Root of hemlock digg'd i' the dark" is one of the ingredients in the witches' cauldron in *Macbeth*, and the hemlock's name has always been one to conjure with, which may account for the fact that several kindred, but less eminent plants unlawfully aspire to it, and are erroneously thus classed. But the true hemlock is unmistakable: the stout bloodspotted stem distinguishes it from the lesser crew; its finely cut fernlike leaves are exceedingly beautiful; and it is of stately habit—I have seen it growing to the height of nine feet, or more, in places where the surrounding brushwood had to be overtopped.

Let us give their due, then, to these outlaws of whom I have spoken, these Robin Hoods of the floral world. Bandits and highwaymen they may be; but after all, our woods and waysides would be much duller if they were banished.

# XX
## SOME MARSH-DWELLERS

WHAT Thoreau wrote of his Massachusetts swamps is hardly less true of ours; a marsh is everywhere a great allurement for botanists. By a road which crosses a certain Sussex Common there is a church, and close behind the church a narrow swampy piece of ground known as "the great bog," which has all the appearance of being waste and valueless; yet whenever I visit the place I think of Thoreau's words: "*My* temple is the swamp." For that bog, ignored or despised by the dwellers round the Common, except when a horse or a cow gets stuck in it and has to be hauled out with ropes, is sacred ground to the flower-lover, as being the home not only of a number of characteristic plants—lesser skull-cap, sundew, bog-bean, bog-asphodel, marsh St. John's-wort, and the scarcer species of marsh bedstraw—but of one of our rarest and most beautiful gentians, the Calathian violet, known and esteemed by the old herbalists as the "marsh-felwort."

The attention of anyone whose thoughts are attuned to flowers must at once be arrested by the colouring of this splendid plant, for its large funnel-shaped blossoms are of the rich gentian blue, striped with green bands, and as it grows not in the bog itself, but on the close-adjoining banks of heather, it is easily accessible. Yet fortunately, in the locality of which I am speaking, it seems to be untouched by those who cross the Common. On the afternoon in early

September when I first found the place, a number of children were blackberrying there, and I dreaded every moment to see them turn aside to pick a bunch of the gentians, which doubtless would soon have been thrown aside to wither, as is the fate of so many spring flowers; but though the blue petals were conspicuous in the heather they were left entirely unmolested. For this merciful abstinence there were probably two reasons: one that the flower-picking habit is exhausted before the autumn; the other that the gentians, however beautiful, are not among the recognized favourites— daffodils, primroses, violets, forget-me-nots, and the like— that by long custom have taken hold of the imagination of childhood. Had it been otherwise, this rare little annual could hardly have survived so long.

In botanical usage there seems to be no difference between the terms "marsh" and "bog," nor need we, I think, follow the rather strained distinction drawn by Anne Pratt, a writer who, though belonging to a somewhat wordy and sentimental school, and indulging in a good deal of what might be called "Anne-prattle," had so real a love of her subject that her best book, *Haunts of the Wild Flowers*, affords very agreeable reading. "The distinction between a bog and a marsh," she says, "is simply that the latter is more wet, and that the foot sinks in; while on a bog the soft soil, though it yields to the pressure of the foot, rises again." The definition itself seems hardly to be based on *terra firma*; but we can fully agree with the writer's conclusion that, at the worst, an adventurous botanist "is often rewarded for the temporary chill by the beauty of the plant which he has gathered." That is a consolation which I have not seldom enjoyed.

But a pleasanter name, in my opinion, than either "marsh" or "bog," is one which is common in the Lake District, and in the northern counties generally, viz. "a moss." It sounds cool and comforting. I recall an occasion when, in the course of a visit to the Newton Regny moss, near Penrith, "the foot sank in," and a good deal more than the foot; but the acquaintance then made for the first time with that giant of the *ranunculus* order, the great spearwort, was sufficient recompense, for who would complain of a wetting when he met with a buttercup four feet in stature?

It so happened, however, that the plant in whose quest I had ventured on the precarious surface of the Newton Regny moss—the great bladderwort—was not to be found on that occasion, though it is reported to make a fine show there in August; possibly, in an early season, it had already finished its flowering, and had sunk, after the inconsiderate manner of its tribe, to the bottom of the pools. Nor did I see its rarer sister, the lesser bladderwort; with whom indeed I have only once had the pleasure of meeting, and that was in a rather awkward place, a deep pond lying close below a railway-bank, and overlooked by the windows of the passing trains, so that I not only had to swim for a flower, but to consult a time-table before swimming, in order to avoid having a "gallery" at the moment when seclusion was desired.

Our North-country "mosses" are indeed temples to the flower-lover, by virtue both of the rarer species that inhabit them, and of the unbroken succession of beautiful plants that they maintain, from the rich gold of the globe-flower in early summer to the exquisite purity of the grass of Parnassus in autumn. Among these bog-plants there is one which to me is very fascinating, though writers are often content to describe its strange purple blossoms as "dingy"—I allude to that wilder relative of the wild strawberry, the marsh-cinquefoil, which, though rather local, is in habit decidedly gregarious. For several years it had eluded me in a Carnarvonshire valley; until one day, wandering by the riverside, I came upon a swampy expanse where it was growing in hundreds, remarkable both for the deep rusty hue of its petals, and for the large strawberry-like fruit that was just beginning to form.

Apart from the more extensive "mosses," the lower slopes of the mountains, both in Cumberland and Wales, are often rich in flowers unsuspected by the wayfarer, who, keeping to some upland track, sees nothing on either side but bare peaty moors that appear to be entirely barren. And barren in many cases they are. You may wander for miles and not see a flower; then suddenly perhaps, on rounding a rock, you will find yourself in one of these natural gardens in the wilderness, where the ground is pink with red rattle growing so thickly as to hide the grass; or white with spotted orchis, handsomer and in greater abundance than is dreamed of in the south; or, a still more glorious sight, tinged over large spaces with the yellow of the bog-asphodel, a plant which is beautiful in its fruit as well as its flower, for when the blossoms are passed the dry wiry stems turn to deep orange. Sun-dews are everywhere; the quaint and affable butterwort is plastered over the wet rocks; and the marsh St. John's-wort, so unlike the rest of its family that the relationship is not always recognized, is frequent in the spongy pools.

Here and there, a small patch of pink on the grey heath, will be seen the delicate bog-pimpernel, which might take rank as the fairest flower of the marsh, were it not that the diminutive ivy-leaved campanula is also trailing its fairy-like form through the wet grasses, among which it might wholly escape notice unless search were made for it. To realize the perfection of its beauty—the exquisite structure of its small green leaves, slender thread-like stems, and bells of palest blue—you must go down on your knees to examine it, however damp the ground; a fitting act of homage to one of the loveliest of Flora's children.

Better cultivation, preceded by improved drainage, is ceaselessly encroaching on our marshlands and lessening the number of their flowers. The charming little cranberry, for instance, once so plentiful that it came to market in wagonloads from the fens of the eastern counties, is now far from common; and our cranberry-tarts have to be supplied from oversea. But much more ravishing than the red berries are the rose-coloured flowers, though they are known to scarcely one in a thousand of the persons familiar with the fruit. I always think with pleasure of the day when I first saw them, on the Whinlatter pass, near Keswick, their small wiry stems creeping on the surface of the swamp, a feast for an epicure's eye. It is under the open air, not under a pie-crust, that such dainties are appreciated as they deserve.

These, then, being some of the many attractions offered by our "mosses," is it surprising that the lover of flowers should play the part of a modern "moss-trooper," and ride out over the border in search for such imperishable spoil? His part, indeed, is a much wiser one than that of the old freebooters; for who would risk life in the forcible lifting of other persons' cattle, when at the slight expense to which Anne Pratt alluded—the temporary chill caused by the sinking of his foot in a marsh—he can enrich himself far more agreeably in the manner which I have described?

# XXI
# A NORTHERN MOOR

A FIRST glance at the bleak and inhospitable moorland of Upper Teesdale would not lead one to suppose that it is famous for its flora. No more desolate-looking upland could be imagined; the great wolds stretch away monotonously, broken only by a few scars that overhang the course of the stream, and devoid of the grandeur that is associated with mountain scenery. No houses are visible, except a few white homesteads that dot the slopes—their whiteness, it is said, being of service to the farmers when they return in late evening from some distant market and are faced with the difficulty of finding their own doors. Its wildness is the one charm of the place; in that it is unsurpassed.

But this bare valley, botanically regarded, is a bit of the far North, interpolated between Durham, Westmorland, and Yorkshire, where the Teesdale basalt or "whinstone" affords an advanced station[Pg 152] for many rare plants of the highland type as they trend southward; and there, for five or six miles, from the upper waterfall of Caldron Snout to that of High Force, the banks of the Tees, with the rough pastures, scars, and fells that form its border, hold many floral treasures.

The first flower to attract attention on these wild lawns is that queen of violets, the mountain pansy (*viola lutea*), not uncommon on many midland and northern heaths, but nowhere else growing in such prodigality as here, or with such rich mingling of colours—orange yellow, creamy white, deep purple, and velvet black—till the eye of the traveller is sated with the gorgeous tints. To the violet tribe this pansy stands in somewhat the same relation as does the bird's-eye primrose to the *primulas*; it is a mountain cousin, at once hardier and more beautiful than its kinsfolk of wood and plain. Seeing it in such abundance, we can understand why Teesdale has been described as "the gardener's paradise;" but the expression is not a fitting one, for "gardener" suggests "trowel," and the nurseryman is the sort of Peri to whom the gates of this paradise ought to be for ever closed.

But perhaps the first stroll which a visitor to Upper Teesdale is likely to take, is by the bank of the river just above High Force; and here the most conspicuous plant is a big cinquefoil, the *potentilla fruticosa*, a shrub about three feet in height, bearing large yellow flowers. Rare elsewhere, it is in exuberance beside the Tees; and I remember the amused surprise with which a dalesman regarded me, when he saw my interest in a weed that to him was so familiar and so cheap.

But the smaller notabilities of the district have to be personally searched for; they do not obtrude themselves on the wayfarer's glance. On the Yorkshire side of the stream stands Cronkley Scar, a buttress of the high moor known as Mickle Fell; and here, in the wet gullies, may be found such choice northern plants as the Alpine meadow-rue; the Scottish asphodel (*Tofieldia*), a small relative of the common bog-asphodel; and the curious viviparous bistort, another highland immigrant, bearing a spike of dull white flowers and small bulbs below.

The fell above the scar is a desolate tract, frequented by golden plover and other moorland birds. On one occasion when I ascended it I was overtaken by a violent storm of wind and rain, which compelled me to leave the further heights of Mickle Fell unexplored, and to retreat to the less exposed pastures of Widdibank on the opposite side of the Tees, here a broad but shallow mountain stream, which in dry weather can be forded without difficulty but becomes a roaring torrent after heavy rains. In the course of two short visits, one in mid-July, the other in the spring of the following year, I twice had the opportunity of seeing the river in either mood, first in unruffled tranquillity, then in furious spate.

It is in May or early June that Teesdale is at the height of its glory; for the plant which lends it a special renown is the spring gentian, perhaps the brightest jewel among all British flowers, small, but a true Alpine, and of that intense blue which signalizes the gentian race. Here this noble flower grows in plenty, not in wide profusion like the pansies, but in large and thriving colonies, not confined to one side of the stream. It was on the Durham bank that I first saw it—one of those rare scenes that a flower-lover cannot forget, for the blue gentians were intermingled with pink bird's-eye primroses, only less lovely than themselves, and close by were a few spikes of the Alpine bartsia, whose sombre purple was in marked contrast with the brilliant hues of its companions.

Of this rare bartsia I had plucked a single flower on my previous visit to the same spot, but then in somewhat hurried circumstances. I had been crossing the wide pastures near Widdibank farm in company with a friend, who, having heard rumours of the temper of Teesdale bulls, had unwisely allowed his thoughts to be somewhat distracted from the pansies. We were in the middle of a field of vast extent, when I heard my companion asking anxiously: "Is *that* one?" It certainly *was* one; not a pansy, but a bull; and he was advancing towards us with very unfriendly noises and gestures. We therefore retired as quickly as we could, without seeming to run—he slowly following us—in the direction of the river; and there, under a high bank, over which we expected every moment the bulky head to reappear, I saw the Alpine bartsia, and stooped to pick one as we fled, my friend mildly deprecating even so slight a delay.

Now, however, on my second visit, I was able to examine the bank at my leisure, and to have full enjoyment of as striking a group of flowers as could be seen on English soil— gentian, bird's-eye primrose, Alpine bartsia—and as if these were not sufficient, the mountain pansy running riot in the pasture just above.

So far, I have spoken only of the plants which I myself saw; there are other and greater rarities in Teesdale which the casual visitor can hardly expect to encounter. The yellow marsh-saxifrage (*S. hirculus*) occurs in two or three places on the slopes of Mickle Fell; so, too, in limestone crevices does the mountain-avens (*dryas octopetala*), and the winter- green (*pyrola secunda*); while on Little Fell, which lies further to the south-west, towards Appleby, the scarce Alpine forget- me-not is reported to be plentiful. I was told by a botanist that, in crossing the moors from Teesdale to Westmorland, he once picked up what he took for a fine clump of the common star-saxifrage, and afterwards found to his surprise that it was the Alpine snow-saxifrage (*S. nivalis*), which during the past thirty years has become exceedingly rare both in the Lake District and in North Wales.

The haunts of the rarer flowers are not likely to be discovered in a day or two, nor yet in a week or two: it is only to him who has gone many times over the ground that such secrets will disclose themselves; but even the passing rambler must be struck, as I was, by the number of noteworthy plants that Teesdale wears, so to speak, upon its sleeve. The globe-flower revels in the moist meadows; so, too, do the water-avens and the marsh-cinquefoil, nor is the butterfly orchis far to seek; and though the yellow marsh-saxifrage may remain hidden, there is no lack of the yellow saxifrage of the mountain (*saxifraga aizoides*), to console you, if it can, for the absence of its rarer cousin. The cross-leaved bedstraw (*galium boreale*), another North-country plant, luxuriates on low wet cliffs by the river.

Last, but not least, in the later months of summer, is the mountain thistle (*carduus heterophyllus*), or the "melancholy thistle" as it is often called—a title which seems to have small relevance, unless all plants of a grave and dignified bearing are to be so named. Do men expect to gather figs of thistles, that they should demand the simple gaiety of the cowslip or the primrose from such a plant as this, whose rich purple flowers, spineless stem, and large parti-coloured leaves— deep green above, white below—mark it as one of the most handsome, as it is certainly the most gracious and benevolent of its tribe?

As I walked down the valley, on a wet morning in July, to take train at Middleton, twenty-four hours of rain had turned the river through which I had easily waded on the previous day, into a flood that was terrifying both in aspect and sound. It was no time for flower-hunting; but even then the wonders of the place were not exhausted; for along the hedgerows I saw in plenty that same stately thistle, which in most districts where it occurs is viewed with some interest and curiosity, but in Teesdale is a roadside weed—subject, I was shocked to observe, to the insolence of the passers-by, who, knowing not what they do, maltreat it as if it were some vulgar pest of the fields, a thing to be hacked at and trampled on. Even so, I saw in it a discrowned king, who "nothing common did or mean."

## XXII
## APRIL IN SNOWDONIA

So wrote De Quincey in one of his finest dream-fugues. There seems, in truth, to be a certain fitness in the turning of men's thoughts at the spring season to the heights of the mountains, where, as nowhere else, the cares and ailments of the winter time are forgotten; and it is a noticeable fact that these upland districts are now as thronged with visitors during Easter week as in August itself. As I write, I am sitting by a wood fire under a high rock in a sheltered nook at Capel Curig, with a biting north-easter blowing overhead and an occasional snow-squall whitening the hillsides around, while the upper ridges are covered in places with great fields and spaces of snow, which at times loom dim and ghostly through the haze, and then gleam out gloriously in the interludes of sunshine. The scenery at the top of Snowdon, the Glyders, Carnedd Llewelyn, and the other giants of the district has been quite Alpine in character. The wind has drifted the snow in great pillowy masses among the rocks, or piled it in long cornices along the edges, and on several days when the air was at its keenest, the snow fields have been crisp and firm, and have afforded excellent footing as a change from the rough "screes" and crags; at other times, when the sun has shone out warmly, the snow has been soft and treacherous, and the spectacle has often been seen of the too trustful tourist struggling waistdeep.

Mid-April in Snowdonia, when March has been cold and wet, shows scarcely an advance from midwinter as far as the blossoming of flowers is concerned. Down by the coast the land is gay with gorse and primroses, but in the bleak upland dales that radiate from the great mountains hardly a bloom is to be seen; nor do the river banks and marshy pastures as yet show so much as a kingcup, a spearwort, or a celandine. The visitors have come in their multitudes to walk, to climb, to cycle, to motor, to take photographs, or to take fish, as the case may be; but if one of them were to confess that he had come to look for flowers he would indeed surprise the natives—still more if he were to point to the upper ramparts of the mountains, among the rocks and snows and clouds, as the place of his design.

Yet it is there that we must climb, if we would see the pride of the purple saxifrage, the earliest of our mountain flowers, blest by botanists with the cumbrous name of *saxifraga oppositifolia*, and often grown by gardeners, who know it as a Swiss immigrant, but not as a British native. A true Alpine, it is not found in this country much below 2,000 feet, and in Switzerland its range is far higher, for it is a neighbour and a lover of the snows. Small and slight as it may seem, when compared with some of its more splendid brethren of the Alps, it has the distinction of a high-bred race, the character of the genuine mountaineer. It is a wearer of the purple, in deed as well as in name.

But our approach to the home of the saxifrage is not to be accomplished without toil, in weather which is a succession of boisterous squalls. Under such a gale we have literally to push our way in a five-mile walk to the foot of the hills, and as we climb higher and higher up the slopes we have a ceaseless tussle with the strong, invisible foe who buffets us from every side in turn, while he hisses against the sharp edges of the crags, or growls with dull subterranean noises under the piles of fallen rocks. As for the streams, they are blown visibly out of their steep channels and carried in light spray across the hillside, while sheets of water are lifted from the surface of the lake. Not till we reach the base of the great escarpment which forms the north-east wall of the mountain are we able to draw breath in peace; for there, under the topmost precipices, flecked with patches of snow, is a strange and blissful calm. But now, just when our search begins, the mists, which have long been circling overhead, creep down and fill the upland hollow where we stand, cutting off our view not only of the valley below but of the range of cliffs above, and confining us in a sequestered cloudland of our own. Still climbing along a line of snowdrifts which follows a ridge of rocks, and which serves at once as a convenient route for an ascent and a safe guide for a return, we scan the likely-looking corners and crevices for the object of our pilgrimage. At first in vain; and then fears begin to assail us that we may be doomed to disappointment. Can we have come too early, even for so early a plant, in a backward season? Or have some wandering tourists or roving knights of the trowel (for such there are) robbed the mountain-side of its gem—for this saxifrage, owing to the brightness of its petals on the grey and barren slopes, is so conspicuous as to be at the mercy of the passer-by.

But even as we stand in doubt there is a gleam of purple through the mist, and yonder, on a boss of rock, is a cluster of the rubies we have come not to steal but to admire. What strikes one about the purple saxifrage, when seen at close quarters, its many bright flowerets peering out from a cushion of moss, is the largeness of the blossoms in proportion to the shortness of the stems; a precocious, wide-browed little plant, it looks as if the cares of existence at these wintry altitudes had given it a somewhat thoughtful cast. At a distance it makes a splash of colour on the rocks, and from the high cliffs above it hangs out, here and there, in tufts that are fortunately beyond reach.

Having paid our homage to the flower, we leave it on its lofty throne among the clouds, and descend by snow-slopes and scree-slides to the windy, blossomless valley beneath. A month hence, when the season of the Welsh poppy, the globe-flower, and the butterwort is beginning, the reign of the purple saxifrage will be at an end. To be appreciated as it deserves, it must be seen not as a poor captive of cultivation, but in its free, wild environment, among the remotest fastnesses of the mountains.

The wild animal life on the hills, so noteworthy in the later spring, seems as yet to have hardly awakened. We saw a white hare one afternoon on Carnedd Llewelyn, but that was the only beast of the mountains that crossed our path during eight days' climbing, nor were the birds so numerous as might have been expected. The croak of the raven was heard at times, in his high breeding-places, and on another occasion there was a triple conflict in the air between a raven, a buzzard, and a hawk. On the lower moorlands the curlew was beginning to arrive from his winter haunts by the seashore, and small flocks of gulls, driven inland by the winds, were hovering over the waters of Llyn Ogwen, where we saw several of them mobbing a solitary heron, who seemed much embarrassed by their onslaught, until he succeeded in getting his great wings into motion.

But if bird-life is still somewhat dormant in these lofty regions, there have been plenty of human migrants on the wing. From our high watch-tower, we saw daily, far below us, the long line of motorists—those terrestrial birds of prey—speeding along the white roads, and flying past a hundred entrancing spots, as if their object were to see as little as possible of what they presumably came to see. Flocks of cyclists, too, were visible here and there, avoiding the cars as best they could, and drinking not so much "the wind of their own speed," in the poet's words, as the swirl and dust of the motors; while on the bypaths and open hillsides swarmed the happier foot-travellers, pilgrims in some cases from long distances over the mountains, or skilled climbers with ropes coiled over their shoulders and faces set sternly towards some beetling crag or black gully in the escarpment above. In one respect only are they all alike—that they are birds of passage and are here only for the holiday. Soon they will be gone, and then the ancient silence will settle down once more upon the hills, and buzzard and raven will be undisturbed, until July and August bring the great summer incursion.

# XXIII
## FLOWER-GAZING *IN EXCELSIS*

THERE is no more inspiring pastime than flower-gazing under the high crags of Snowdon. The love of flowers reveals a new and delightful aspect of the mountain life, and leads its votaries into steeps and wilds which, as they lie aloof from the usual ways of the climber, might otherwise escape notice. It must be owned that our Cumbrian and Cambrian hills are not rich in flowers as Switzerland is rich; one cannot here step out on the mountain-side and see great sheets of colour, as on some Alpine slope; and not only must we search for our treasures, but we must know *where* to search. They do not grow everywhere; much depends on the nature of the soil, much on the altitude, much on the configuration of the hills. There are great barren tracts which bear little but heather and bilberry; but there are rarer beds of volcanic ash and cal careous rock which are a joy to the heart of the flower-lover.

Again, one is apt to think that on those heights, where the winter is long and severe, it is the southern flanks that must be the haunt of the flowers; in reality, it is the north-east side that is the more favoured, owing to the fact that the hills, in both districts, for the most part rise gently from the south or the south-west, in gradual slopes that are usually dry and wind-swept, while northward and eastward they fall away steeply in broken and water-worn escarpments. It is here, among the wet ledges and rock-faces, constantly sprayed from the high cliffs above, where springs have their sources, that the right conditions of shade and moisture are attained; and here only can the Alpines be found in any abundance. The precipices of Cwm Idwal and Cwm Glas, in Wales, and in the Lake District the east face of Helvellyn, may stand as examples of such rock-gardens.

The course of a climber is usually along the top of the ridge, that of the botanist at its base; his paradise is that less frequented region which may be called the undercliff, where the "screes" begin to break away from the overhanging precipice, and where, in the angle thus formed, there is often a little track which winds along the hillside, sometimes rising, sometimes falling, but always with the cliff above and the scree-slope below. Following this natural guidance he may scramble around the base of the rocks, or along their transverse ledges, and feast his eyes on the many mountain flowers that are within sight, if not within reach.

It is a fine sport, this flower-gazing; not only because all the plants are beautiful and many of them rare, but because it demands a certain skill to balance oneself on a steep declivity, while looking upward, through binoculars, at some attractive clump of purple saxifrage, or moss-campion, or thrift, or rose-root, or globe-flower, as the case may be.

To the veteran rambler especially, this flower-cult is congenial; for it supplies—I will not say an excuse for not going to the top, but a less severe and exacting diversion, which still takes him into the inmost solitudes of the mountain, and keeps him in unfailing touch with its character and genius.

I have spoken of Snowdonia in the spring; let us view it now in the fulness of June or July, when its flora is at its richest. It is not till you have climbed to a height of about two thousand feet that the true joys of the mountains begin. At first, perhaps, as you follow the course of the stream you will see nothing more than a bunch of white scurvy-grass or a spray of golden-rod; but when you reach the region where the thin cascade comes sliding down over the moist rocks, and the topmost cliffs seem to impend, then you will have your reward, for you have entered into the kingdom of the Alpines.

Suppose, for example, that you stand at the foot of the narrow ridge of Crib-y-Ddysgl, a great precipice which overhangs the upper chambers of Cwm Glas on the northern side of Snowdon, with an escarpment formed of huge slabs of rock intersected by wet gullies, narrow niches, and transverse terraces of grass. Looking up, to where the Crib towers above, you will see a goodly array of plants. Thrift is there, in large clumps as handsome as on any sea-cliffs; rose-root, the big mountain-stonecrop; cushions of moss-campion, which bears the local name of "Snowdon pink"; lady's-mantle, intermixed with the reddening leaves of mountain-sorrel; Welsh poppy, not so common a flower in Wales as its name would suggest; and at least three kinds of beautiful white blossoms—the starry saxifrage, the mossy saxifrage, and the shapely little sandwort (*arenaria verna*), as fair as the saxifrages themselves, and what higher praise could be given? The flower-lover can scarcely hope for greater delight than that which the starry saxifrage will yield him. It has been well said that "one who has not seen it growing, say, in some rift of the rock exposed by the wearing of the mountain torrent, cannot imagine how lovely it is, or how fitly it is named. White and starry, and saxifrage—how charming must that which has three such names be!"

Another lofty rock-face, similar in its flora to that of Snowdon, is the precipice at the head of Cwm Idwal, near the point where it is broken by the famous chasm of the Devil's Kitchen. Hereabouts is the chief station of the *Lloydia*, or spiderwort, a rather rare and pretty Alpine, a delicate lily of the high rocks, bearing solitary white flowers veined with red, and a few exceedingly narrow leaves that resemble the legs of a spider. Unlike most mountain plants, it has a considerable local reputation; and during its short flowering season in June one may observe small parties of enthusiasts from Bangor or Carnarvon, diligently scanning the black cliffs above Llyn Idwal, in the hope of spying it. The place where I first saw the *Lloydia* in blossom was Cwm Glas; but I had previously noticed its long thin leaves in two or three places around the Devil's Kitchen.

The haunts of the Alpine meadow-rue (*thalictrum alpinum*) are similar to those of the spiderwort; and a most elegant little plant it is, its gracefully drooping terminal cluster of small yellowish flowers being borne on a simple naked stem, whereas its less aristocratic relative, the smaller meadow-rue (*t. collinum*), which is much commoner on these rocks, is bushier and more branched. I had many disappointments, before I rightly apprehended the true Alpine species; once distinguished, it cannot again be mistaken.

It was to a chance meeting in Ogwen Cottage, at the foot of Cwm Idwal, with Dr. Lloyd Williams, a skilled botanist who had brought a party of friends to visit the home of the *Lloydia*, that I owed my introduction to another very beautiful inhabitant of those heights, the white mountain-avens, known to rock-gardeners as *dryas octopetala*. Happy is the flower-gazer who has looked on the galaxy, the "milky way," of those fair mountain nymphs—for the plant is in truth an oread rather

126

than a dryad—where they shed their lustre from certain favoured ledges in a spot which it is safer to leave unspecified. I must have passed close to the place many scores of times, in the forty or more years during which I had known the mountain; yet never till then did I become aware of the treasure that was enshrined in it!

But of all the glories of Cwm Idwal—rarities apart—the greatest, when the summer is at its prime, is the array of globe-flowers. This splendid buttercup usually haunts the banks of mountain streams, or the sides of damp woods, in the West country and the North; its range is given in the *Flora of the Lake District* as not rising above nine hundred feet; but in Snowdonia, not content to dwell with its cousins the kingcups and spearworts in the upland valleys, it aspires to a far more romantic station, and is seen blooming in profusion at twice and almost three times that height on the most precipitous rock-ledges. One may gaze by the hour, enraptured, and never weary of the sight.

I have by no means exhausted the list of notable Snowdonian flowers that are native in the two localities of which I have spoken, or in a few other spots that are similarly favoured by geological conditions: the sea-plantain, the mountain-cudweed, the stone-bramble, the queer little whitlow-grass with twisted pods (*draba incana*), its still rarer congener the Alpine rock-cress, and the *Saussurea*, or Alpine saw-wort—all these, and more, are to be found there by the pilgrim who devotedly searches the scriptures of the hills. But of the *Saussurea* some mention will have to be made in the next chapter; for it is now time to turn from Cambria to Cumbria, from the "cwms" and "cribs" of Snowdon to the "coves" and "edges" of Helvellyn.

# XXIV
## COVES OF HELVELLYN

So far I have spoken more of the Welsh mountain flowers than of those belonging to Lakeland; but the difference between the two districts, in regard to their respective floras, is not very great, and with a few exceptions the plants that are native on the one range may be looked for on the other. The *Lloydia* is found in Snowdonia only; and Wales can boast, not a monopoly, but a greater plenty of the moss-campion and the purple saxifrage. On the other hand, the Alpine lady's-mantle and the yellow mountain-saxifrage, both abundant in Cumberland, are absent from Carnarvonshire; and this is somewhat of a loss, for the common lady's-mantle, charming though it is, lacks the beauty of the Alpine, and the yellow saxifrages, as they hang from the rocks like a phalanx of tiny golden shields—each with bright petals and pale green sepals radiating from a central boss—are among the greatest ornaments of the fells.

Again, the lovely little bird's-eye primrose is a North-country plant which is not found in Wales; against which may be set, perhaps, that gem of the damp mosses on certain Welsh streamsides, the ivy-leaved bell-flower. More characteristic of Lakeland than of Snowdonia, though not peculiar to it, are those two very beautiful flowers, the one a child of the swamp, the other of the high pastures, the grass of Parnassus, and the mountain-pansy; and to conclude the list, the snow-saxifrage and the mountain-avens are about equally rare in both countries—the avens, indeed, is confined to one or two stations, where fortunately it is little known.

Helvellyn, as a mountain, is very inferior to Snowdon, nor indeed can it compete in grandeur with its own Cumbrian neighbours, the Great Gable and Scafell; but among visitors to the Lakes it has nevertheless an enduring reputation, largely due to the poems in which Scott and Wordsworth have sung its praises. Accordingly, during the tourist season, the anxious question: "Is that Helvellyn?" may often be overheard; and on a fine day all sorts of incongruous persons may be seen making their way up the weary slopes that lead from Grasmere to its crest. I once observed a gentleman in a top-hat toiling upward in the queue; on another occasion I witnessed at the summit a violent quarrel between a married couple, the point of dispute (on which they appealed to me) being whether their little dog was, or was not, in danger of being blown over the cliffs. As the west wind was certainly very strong, and Helvellyn had already been associated with the story of a dog's fidelity, I ventured to advise a retreat.

On the east side, however, where its "dark brow" overlooks the Red Tarn, and throws out two great lateral ridges—on the right, in De Quincey's words, "the awful curtain of rock called Striding Edge," and Swirrel Edge on the left—Helvellyn is a very fine mountain, and what is more to the present purpose, is botanically the most interesting of all the Lakeland fells. From Grisedale Tarn to Keppelcove, a distance of full three miles, that great escarpment, with the several "coves" that nestle beneath it, is the home of many rare Alpine flowers, corresponding in that respect with the Welsh rock-faces of Idwal and Cwm Glas; and though it does not offer so conspicuous a display, or such keen inducements to flower-gazing, a search along its narrow ledges, and under the impending crags, home of the hill fox, will seldom disappoint the adventurer.

Some years ago I spent a week of July, in two successive seasons, at Patterdale, for the purpose of becoming better acquainted with the mountain flowers, but on both occasions the weather was very stormy and made it difficult to be on the fells. At first I searched chiefly under Striding Edge and the steep front of Helvellyn, among the rocks that lie behind the Red Tarn, and in similar places above Keppelcove Tarn in the adjoining valley, hoping with good luck to light on the snow-saxifrage. In this I was unsuccessful; but I twice found a plant I had not hitherto met with—in appearance a small spineless thistle, with a cluster of light-purple scented flowers—which proved to be the Alpine saw-wort, or *Saussurea*, and which in later years I saw again on Snowdon. A blossom which I picked and kept for several months was so little affected by its separation from the parent stem that it continued its vital processes in a vase, and passed from flowering to seeding without interruption. Like the orpine, it was a veritable "live-long," or as the politicians say, "die-hard."

At Patterdale I was so fortunate as to make the acquaintance of Mr. Robert Nixon, a resident who has had a long and intimate knowledge of the local flora; and he very kindly devoted a day to showing me some of his flower-haunts on Helvellyn. In the course of this expedition, one of the pleasantest in my memory, a number of interesting plants were noted by us: among them the mountain-pansy; the cross-leaved bedstraw; the vernal sandwort; the Alpine meadow-rue; the moss-campion; the purple saxifrage, now past flowering; the mountain willow-herb (*epilobium alsinifolium*), not the true Alpine willow-herb, but a native of similar places among the higher rills; and the *salix herbacea*, or "least willow," the smallest of British trees, which[Pg 175]when growing on the bare hill-tops is not more than two inches in height, though in the clefts of rock at the edge of the main escarpment we found it of much larger size.

The moss-campion (*silene acaulis*) is especially associated with the locality of which I am speaking—the neighbourhood of Grisedale Tarn—and is mentioned in the "Elegiac Verses," composed by Wordsworth "near the mountain track that leads from Grasmere through Grisedale":

There cleaving to the ground, it lies,

With multitude of purple eyes,

Spangling a cushion green like moss.

To this the poet added in a note: "This most beautiful plant is scarce in England. The first specimen I ever saw of it, in its native bed, was singularly fine, the tuft or cushion being at least eight inches in diameter. I have only met with it in two places among our mountains, in both of which I have since sought for it in vain." The other place may have been the hill above Rydal Mount; for a contributor to the *Flora of the Lake District* states that it was there shown to him by Wordsworth. The poet's knowledge of the higher mountains, and of the mountain flora, was not great. The moss-campion though local, is much less rare than he supposed, and its "cushions" grow to a far larger bulk than that of the one described by him. In his*Holidays on High Lands* (1869), Macmillan, paying tribute to the beauty of this flower, remarks that "a sheet of it last summer on one of the Westmorland mountains measured five feet across, and was one solid mass of colour." I have seen it approaching that size in Wales.

Another plant which I was anxious to see was the Alpine *cerastium* (mouse-ear chickweed), said to grow "sparingly" on the crags of Striding Edge and in a few other places. I failed to find it; but when Mr. Nixon had pointed out to me, in a photograph of the Edge, a particular crag on which he had noticed the flower in a previous summer, I determined to renew the search. This the weather prevented; but in the following year, happening to be in Borrowdale in June, I walked from Keswick to the top of Helvellyn, and thence descended to Striding Edge, where, on the very rock indicated by Mr. Nixon, I found the object of my journey—not yet in flower, for I was somewhat ahead of its season, but authenticated as *cerastium alpinum* by the small oval leaves covered with dense white down. I have several times seen, high up on Carnedd Llewelyn, a form of *cerastium* with larger flowers than the common kind; this I think must have been what is called *c. alpestre* in the*Flora of Carnarvonshire*; but the true *alpinum*, though frequent in the Scottish highlands, is decidedly rare in Wales.

Even when the summer is far spent, there is hope for the flower-lover among these mountains, especially if he penetrate into one of those deep fissures—more characteristic of the Scafell range than of Helvellyn—known locally as "gills": I have in mind the upper portion of Grain's Gill, near the summit of the Sty Head Pass, where, on an autumn day, one may still see, on either bank of the chasm, a goodly array of flowers. Most prevalent, perhaps, are the satiny leaves of the Alpine lady's-mantle, which is extraordinarily abundant in this part of the Lake District, and forms a thick green carpet on many of the slopes. Against this background stand out conspicuously tall spires of golden-rod, rich cushions of wild thyme, and clumps of white sea-campion, a shore plant which, like thrift, sea-plantain, and scurvy-grass, seems almost equally at home on the heights. There, too, are the mountain-sorrel, and rose-root; butterworts, with leaves now faded to a sickly yellow; tufts of harebell, northern bedstraw and hawkweed; stout stalks of angelica; and, best of all, festoons of yellow saxifrages, beautiful even in their decay.

## XXV
## GREAT DAYS

I hearing get, who had but ears,
And sight, who had but eyes before;
I moments live, who lived but years.

THOREAU.

IN flower-seeking, as in other sports and sciences, the unexpected is always happening; there are rich days and poor days, surprises and disappointments; the plant which we hailed as a rarity may prove on examination to be but a gay deceiver; and contrariwise, when we think we have come home empty-handed, it may turn out that the vasculum contains some unrecognized treasure; as when, after what seemed to be a barren day on Helvellyn, I found that I had brought back with me the Alpine saw-wort.

That in the study of flowers, as in all natural history, we should be more attracted by the rare than by the common is inevitable; it is a tendency that cannot be escaped or denied, but it may at least be kept within bounds, so that familiarity shall not breed the proverbial contempt, nor rarity a vulgar and excessive admiration. The quest for the rare, provided that it does not make us forget that the common is often no less beautiful, or lead to that selfish acquisitiveness which is the bane of "collecting," is a foible harmless in itself and even in some cases useful, as inciting us to further activities.

The sulphur-wort, or "sea hog's-fennel," for instance, is not especially attractive—a big coarse plant, five feet in stature, with a solid stem, uncouth masses of grass-like leaves, and large umbels of yellow flowers—yet I have a gratifying recollection of a visit which I once paid to its haunts on the Essex salt marshes near Hamford Water. Again, the twisted-podded whitlow-grass is a rather shabby-looking little crucifer; but the day when I found it under the crags of Snowdon in Cwm Glas stands out distinguished and unforgotten. It is natural that we should observe more closely what there are fewer opportunities of observing.

Let me speak first of the barren days. An old friend of mine who is of an optimistic temperament once assured me for my comfort, that the flower-seeker must not feel discouraged if he fail in his pursuit; since it is not from mere success, but from the effort itself, that benefit is derived. The text should run, not "Seek, and ye shall find," but, "Seek, and ye shall not *need* to find." This may be a true doctrine, but it seems rather a hard one; certainly it is not easy, at the time, to regard with entire complacency the result of a blank day; and that there will be blank days is beyond doubt, for it is strange how long some of the "wanted" plants, the De Wets of the floral world, will evade discovery. I have looked into the face of many hundreds of star-saxifrages on the hills of Wales and Cumberland, but have never yet set eyes upon its rare sister, the snow or "clustered" saxifrage. In like manner among the innumerable flowers of the chalk fields, in the South, that elusive little annual, the mouse-tail, has hitherto remained undetected. So, too, with many other rarities: the list of the found may increase year by year, but that of the *un*found is never exhausted.

It is well that it is so, and that satiety cannot chill the ardour of the flower-lover, but like Ulysses, "always roaming with a hungry heart," he has ever before him an object for his pursuit. "Wretched is he," says Rousseau, "who has nothing left to wish for." Nor is the reward a merely figurative one, such as that of the husbandmen in the fable, who, after digging the ground in search of a buried treasure, were otherwise recompensed; for the lean days are happily interspersed with the fat days, and to the botanist there is surely no joy on earth like that of discovering a flower that is new to him; it is a thrilling event which compensates tenfold for all the failures of the past.

Very remarkable, too, is the freakishness of fortune, which often, while denying what you crave, will toss you something quite different and unlooked for: I remember how when searching vainly for the spider orchis at the foot of the Downs in Kent, I stumbled on an abundance of the "green man." Or perhaps, just at the moment when you are relinquishing the quest as hopeless, and have put it wholly from your mind, you will be startled to see the very flower that you sought.

Burningly it came on me all at once!
Dotard, a-dozing at the very nonce,
After a life spent training for the sight!

As Thoreau expressed it: "What you seek in vain for, half your life, one day you come full upon, all the family at dinner."

But the great days! I have sometimes fancied that in those enterprises which are to mark the finding of a new flower, one has an inner anticipation, a sense of hopefulness and quiet satisfaction that on ordinary occasions is lacking. But this assurance must be an instinctive one; it is useless to affect a confidence that does not naturally arise; for though perseverance is essential, any presumptuous attempt to forestall a favourable issue will only lead to discomfiture. Then at last, when the goal is reached, comes the devotee's reward—the knowledge that is won only by attainment, the ecstasy, the moments that are better than years. In this, as in much else, the search for flowers is symbolic of the search for truth.

Nothing, as they say, succeeds like success; and there are times, in this absorbing pursuit, when one piece of good fortune is linked closely with another. I shall not easily forget that day on Snowdon, when, after meeting for the first time with the Alpine meadow-rue, I almost immediately saw my first spiderwort some ten feet above me on the rocky cliff, and reached it by building a cairn of stones against the foot of the precipice to serve me as a ladder.

Among the great days that have fallen to my lot while following the call of the wildflower, one other shall be mentioned—a fair September afternoon when I had wandered for miles about the wide pastures that border the Trent, in what seemed to be a fruitless search for the meadow-saffron. Already it was time to turn on my homeward journey, when I struck into a field from which hay had been carried in the summer; and there, scattered around in large clusters of a score or more together, some lilac, some white, all with a satiny translucence in the warm sunshine which gave them an extraordinary and fairy-like charm, were hundreds of the leafless "autumn crocuses," as they are called, though in fact the flower is more lovely and ethereal than any crocus of the garden. Not the day only, but the place itself was glorified by them; and now of all those spacious but rather desolate Nottinghamshire river-meadows, I remember only that one spot:

I crossed a moor, with a name of its own,
And a certain use in the world, no doubt;
Yet a hand's-breath of it shines alone,
'Mid the blank miles round about.

Nor are all the great days necessarily of that strenuous sort where success can only be achieved by effort; for there are some days which may also be called great, or at least memorable, when one attains by free gift of fortune to what might long have been searched for in vain. I refer to those happy occasions when a friend says: "Look here! I'd like to show you that field where the elecampane grows," or, it may be, the habitat (the only one in England) of the spring snowflake; or the place on Wansfell Pike where the mountain-twayblade lies hidden beneath the heather. Such things have befallen me now and then; nor am I likely to forget the day when Bertram Lloyd took me to the haunt of the creeping toadflax in Oxfordshire; or when, with Sydney Olivier for guide, I emerged from the aisles of Wychwood Forest on to some rough grassy ground, where in company with meadow crane's-bill, clustered bell-flower, and woolly-headed thistle, the blue *salvia pratensis* was flourishing in glorious abundance.

For recollection plays a large part in the flower-lover's enjoyment. Wordsworth and his daffodils are but a trite quotation; yet many hearts besides Wordsworth's have filled with pleasure at the memory of a brave array of flowers, or even of a single gallant plant seen in some wild locality by mountain, meadow, or shore. The great days were not born to be forgotten.

# XXVI
## THE LAST ROSE

And summer's lease hath all too short a date.

THE great days were not born to be forgotten. It is well
that memory should come to the aid of the flower-lover; for
none is more deserving of such comfort than he, keeping
constant watch as he does over the transitoriness of the
seasons, and having prescience of the summer's departure
while summer is still at its height.

> Sometimes a late autumnal thought
> Has crossed my mind in green July.

It is in the prime of the year that such intimations of
mortality are keenest; when the "fall" itself has arrived, there
is less of regret than of resignation. I do not know where the
tranquil grief for parted loveliness is so tenderly expressed as
in a fragmentary poem of Shelley's, "The Zucca," which,
though little known by the majority of readers, contains some
of the most poignant, most Shelleyan verses ever written.
The poet relates how when the Italian summer was dead, and
autumn was in turn expiring, he went forth in grief for the
decay of that ideal beauty—"dim object of my soul's
idolatry"—of which he, above all men, was the worshipper,
and in this mood of sadness found the withered gourd which
was the subject of his song.

> And thus I went lamenting, when I saw
> A plant upon the river's margin lie,
> Like one who loved beyond his Nature's law.

And in despair had cast him down to die.

There is a fitness in such imagery; for flowers seem to serve naturally as emblems of human emotions. Who has not felt the pathos of a faded blossom kept as a memorial of the past? Many years ago I was given a beautifully bound copy of Moxon's edition of *Shelley*; and when I noticed that opposite that loveliest of poems, "Epipsychidion," were a few pink petals interleaved, I was sure that their presence at such a page was not merely accidental; and it has since been a whim of mine that those tokens of some bygone incident in the life of a former owner of the book should not be displaced.

There are vicissitudes in human lives with which flowers become associated in our thoughts. I recall a calm autumn day spent in company with a friend upon the Surrey Downs, when the marjoram and other fragrant flowers of the chalk were still as beautiful as in summer, but the sadness of a near departure from that familiar district lay heavy on my mind; and that day proved indeed to be the end of many happy years, for long afterwards, when I returned to those hills, all was changed for *me*, though Nature was kindly as before. Thus a date, not greatly heeded at the time, may be found to have marked one of life's turning-points, and the flowers connected with it may hold a peculiar significance in memory.

It is a sad moment for a flower-lover when he sees before him "the last rose of summer" ("rose" is a term which may here be used in a general sense for any sweet and pleasing flower), and realizes that he is now face to face with the season's euthanasia, "that last brief resurrection of summer in its most brilliant memorials, a resurrection that has no root in the past, nor steady hold upon the future, like the lambent and fitful gleams from an expiring lamp." Yet so gradual is this change, and the resurrection of which De

Quincey speaks so entrancing, that one is comforted even while he grieves.

For example, there are few sights more cheering on a late September day than to find by some bare tidal river a colony of the marsh-mallow. The most admired member of the family is usually the muskmallow; and certainly it is a very pretty flower, with its bright foliage and the pink satiny sheen of its corolla; but far more charming, though less showy in appearance, is its modest sister of the salt marshes, whose leaves, overspread with hoary down, are soft as softest velvet, and her petals steeped in as tender and delicate a tint of palest rose-colour as could be imagined in dreams. There is something especially gracious about this *althæa*, or "healer"; and her virtues are not more soothing to body than to mind.

It was from the Sussex shingles that I started, and from the same shore my concluding picture shall be drawn—a quaint sea-posy that I picked there on an October afternoon, not so romantic, certainly, as one of violets or forget-me-nots, but in that sere season not less heartening than any nosegay of the spring. It held but three flowers, samphire, sea-rocket, and sea-heath. The samphire, at all times a singular and attractive herb, was now in fruit, and had faded to a wan yellow; the rocket was still in flower, its lilac blossoms crowning the solid glaucous stalk, and its thick fleshy leaves rivalling the texture of seaweed; the small sea-heath, with wiry reddish stems and dark-green foliage, lent itself by a natural contrast for twining around its bulkier companions. Thus grouped they stood for weeks in a vase on my mantel, until the time for wildflowers was past, and the "black and tan" days of winter were already let loose on the earth. And even when the year is actually at its lowest, the sunnier times can be revived and re-enacted in thought; for memory is potent.